BROTHERS

BOOK ONE

Bones

A DARK MAFIA ROMANCE

CHELLE ROSE

NOTE TO THE READER

Your mental health is important. Please don't read blind if you have any triggers! You can find them here:

DEDICATION

If you ordered a tattooed MMC that will do anything to protect his woman, this one's for you. Bones is dark, delicious and dangerous. Three of my four favorite 'D' words. Don't worry, the other one is in this book too!

Chapter One

BONES

Butterflies are meant to be free. I clipped her wings, and broke something that has been broken before. Only the most vile of human beings would take such beauty and crush it beneath their feet. When I was a boy, my mother warned me; 'You can't keep butterflies, Luca. Admire the beauty and then let it go. We don't destroy the things we love.'

Like the pretty blue butterfly all those years ago, I tried to keep her as my captive. My mother was wrong. I do destroy the things I love.

Chapter Two

ATHENA

I look around the motel room, hating my surroundings and hating myself even more, because it's far better than my previous home. It's a small room with a queen sized bed, a tiny end table with a bible on top, and a television that has seen better days. Sometimes it works, but most times it doesn't. My favorite part of the entire room is the window because, while I'm not allowed to go outside unless I'm told to, I can watch the families enjoying life in a way I've never known. Manny opens the door, looking as pissed off as he usually does. Taking a deep breath, I brace myself for what's sure to come. I don't have a clue why he always looks ready to fight, but he does.

"Here's the address of your next job."

I glance at the piece of paper he hands me, and the location means nothing to me. I don't know where I'm going.

Narrowing his gaze at me, he says, "I want the red Lambo."

Has he lost his mind? I've stolen many things for him over the last year: money, jewelry, drugs, but not a car.

I shake my head, knowing I'll anger him. "I can't. Honestly, Manny, I don't even know how."

It's the truth. This is not an item I can simply stuff in a bag and make my exit casually. I've seen people in movies hot-wiring cars, but I don't know how.

With a fierce glare, he walks over to me where I sit on the bed; the fury radiates from his body as he climbs over me and grabs my throat, squeezing so hard I can't breathe.

"You will, *Princess,* unless you prefer to go back to daddy."

He has my number and we both know it. I will do anything to not go back there. Of course, Manny doesn't stop there, he never does. Everybody in my life gets off on causing me pain.

"Do you miss being daddy's little girl?"

Releasing my throat, he laughs loudly and says, "Is that it, Princess? You miss daddy's dick in your mouth?"

"I'll do it, alright. Now stop. Stop saying that shit and stop calling me that."

My sometimes boyfriend laughs even louder and I officially hate him. I didn't end up with him because of an attraction. He isn't bad looking, I suppose, but that's not what drew me to him. His hair and eyes are both dark, he has a square jaw, and skin that appears permanently tanned. I'm sure women find him attractive, but that wasn't what did it for me. Manny offered me a way out of the never ending abuse. And some days I wonder who's worse. Him or my father. Like all abusive men, Manny started out sweet, promising me the world. He'd get me away from my dad and keep me safe. It didn't last long. First, he requested my help with stealing some jewelry, and before I knew it; it was no longer a request. If I don't want to go back to my father's house, I have no choice.

Manny Ortega is an opportunist. He'll take advantage of anything and anyone if it makes him money. He claims to love me, but it's all a lie. I'm nothing more than his cash cow. I steal things for him; he sells them and profits in a big way, sometimes hundreds and oftentimes by the thousands. In return, he rents this cheap motel room for me to stay in and supplies me with food. Kind of. The occasional ramen or loaf of bread with bologna isn't my dream culinary option. He knows, as well as I do, that I'd rather starve to death than to go back to my father. This is why I do everything he tells me to. It's why I'll attempt to steal this *Lamborghini*. Most people would be afraid of getting caught and going to prison.

I'm not.

In fact, I'm hoping for it. A life behind bars would be better than this.

When I get to the house that has this Lambo that Manny wants so badly, I can't believe my eyes. It's dark so I can't see well, but I note how massive this property is. The main house itself appears to be made of white stone. It's gated, and on the front of the black gate is a design of three skulls with wings. And in a circle it has a word I can't read. Other than the metal gate, a tall cement wall surrounds the rest of the house, and it appears the goal is to keep people out. People like me.

This house is isolated, really fucking isolated, and it makes all the hairs stand on the back of my neck. In my experience, people this far out with no one around normally have shit to hide. Like my father. The bile rises in my throat at the not so distant memory of him.

Manny had me dropped off three miles from here, and even that far away, there was no civilization. Which of course means if I'm stealing a car from a serial killer, and get caught, they'll likely never find my body. I snort at myself from my spot in the trees. That would be just my luck, to rob a killer. Would *Dexter* ask why I was stealing from him, and butcher every man in my life who has ever hurt me? Or would I find myself bound to his table?

I approach the large cement wall around the house. It's got to be eight fucking feet tall. How am I supposed to climb that? The sky is black. The property is unnaturally dark. Almost as if I'm walking into a trap. Like someone wants me to think no one is here. Still, I have to get to the garage where I'm sure the precious half a million dollar car is stored.

Climbing up the wall, I immediately fall and know I have no choice but to try again. Chances are good that I won't leave this house without broken bones.

Chapter Three
BONES

This shit night only goes from bad to worse. As I'm pulling up to my house, my head of security calls me, which is never good news.

"What, Eduardo?" I answer with a growl, knowing I'm being an asshole because he never calls me without justification.

"Boss, we have a problem."

I glare at my Bluetooth display as I wait for him to finish.

"There's an intruder trying to scale the wall."

I run a hand through my hair in agitation. "Fucking kill them. All of them."

That's a simple solution. If you come into my home in the middle of the night, you die. Perhaps Eduardo has forgotten this.

"If you wish, Boss, it's just-"

Slamming my hand on the steering wheel, I yell, "Spit it out!"

"It's a woman. She's alone and stuck. And crying."

I laugh obnoxiously. I'm equally irritated and curious.

"Women cry, Eduardo. It's what they fucking do. Stand down and let me do your job. Where is she?"

"The East wall, sir."

After hanging up, I exit my vehicle and walk through my gate to approach the east wall. It's not common for people to attempt to get on to my property because it's virtually impossible. Ten-foot cement walls with barbed wire discourage it. And anybody in our criminal world knows I have security. They don't see them for a reason, but they are always there. Always watching. And never has the idiot been a woman. *Oh fuck.* Could it be one of my one-night stands? I dismiss the thought almost instantly, because that's a lot of trouble to go through for good dick. It is *really* good dick, but still.

I walk up to the wall, and spot what Eduardo meant about her being stuck. There's enough light to see her, but it's too dark to get a good look. She hangs upside down with her back against the wall, pretty blue-gray eyes wide with fear, as she whimpers like she's in pain. Her shirt is ripped wide open, exposing her tits in a black lacy bra. Her jeans are ripped as well, and her leg bleeds as she hangs helplessly. Barbed wire is a bitch, and normally a deterrent.

I turn my head to get a look at her face. Nope. Don't know her. I'm pretty sure I'd remember her. Long dark hair with soft curls, eyes so blue I can even see them in the dark. High cheekbones and full lips that look as soft as her skin. Without a doubt, this is a woman I'd likely never forget.

Righting myself, I grin at her. "You've got yourself into quite the situation."

Her hair hangs down, nearly touching the ground along with her shredded t-shirt, but she manages to glare at me as if I'm the asshole that tried to get onto *her* property.

"Be a gentleman and help me down."

I chuckle loudly. "You are in no position to make demands. And I assure you, I'm no gentleman."

I'm feeling generous, I suppose, so I grab her pant leg that's hooked on the wire, and yank until she falls free with a thud.

"Fucking asshole," she screams, causing me to chuckle again. Bending down, I pick her up off the ground and throw her over my shoulder. I hold her thighs against my chest as I make it to the back of my house, where my guards open the door for me. The pretty brunette knees my stomach, squealing the entire time, and it's really beginning to piss me off. I walk down the steps into my basement and she calls me an asshole again. Setting her down, I grab her hair and yank her head back painfully. "Call me that again and you'll see what an asshole is."

I let go of her, and she takes a quick look around at her surroundings and suddenly seems very nervous, as she should be. A

8

gasp escapes from her pretty lips when she spots the cage, and then the chains on the wall. Aside from my chair down here, it's empty other than my containment items.

She turns to me, and it's as if I can actually see her lightbulb moment and everything falls into place for her.

"You're not going to let me go."

Her lashes flutter as she raises her eyes to mine, and Jesus, she really is beautiful. I knew that when I first laid eyes on her, but it's more noticeable now that we aren't in the dark. It's going to hurt to kill something so gorgeous, but there's no choice. Fucking stunning. Long dark, wavy hair. Blue-gray eyes, more gray than blue. Pouty lips begging for a dick between them. Pale skin, perky tits with hard nipples poking through her thin bra. A body so feminine. Looking at her now, I know I'm not going to just kill her. It won't be quick. First, I'll break her.

"Are you going to kill me?" She asks in a breathy, trembling voice.

"Yes, Butterfly. I am."

She swallows hard. "Then get on with it."

"First things first. Why were you attempting to break into my house?"

Crossing her arms over her chest, she scowls at me like I've wronged her. "I was not trying to get into your house."

Arching an eyebrow at her, I shake my head. "Climbing ten foot cement walls and getting stuck on barbed wire is a hobby then, Butterfly?"

Had I met her under different circumstances, I'd already be inside her, but unfortunately this time that's not an option.

"Get undressed."

With a roll of her eyes, she surprises me and does as she's told. Why didn't she even try to fight? I lean forward and run my thumb down her bleeding thigh. "Does this hurt?"

9

With a glower, she growls like a tiny kitten. "Why do you care? You're going to kill me, anyway."

I drag my tongue slowly over my thumb, tasting the coppery sweetness of her blood, and she gives me a disgusted face. "I will not give you what you want. If you want to fuck me, you'll need to rape me."

I gaze at her curiously. "I've never raped a woman in my life. I don't need to. And I have no intention of fucking you, Butterfly."

Do I miss the sad look in her eyes? No. But it doesn't matter. She did this to herself.

"Why do you keep calling me that?"

Running my fingers down her cheek, it's like I'm in a trance. "I had a pretty little blue butterfly when I was a boy. You remind me of it. Stunning but fragile. Too fragile for life. One torn little wing, and it's grounded. It can't survive the monsters of its world, if it can't fly. Butterflies are meant to be free. Beautiful and free. One thing you are. The other you never will be."

"I'm not fragile," she roars angrily.

I can't help the grin that overtakes my face. "We shall see, Butterfly. Now get in the cage."

Chapter Four
ATHENA

My legs are like lead, I can't move. I'm naked, afraid, and so goddamn angry as I put the pieces together. He knows my dad. Did Manny set me up? I have spent the last year making sure I never have to go back to my father's house. Glancing at the cage, I know it shouldn't seem as familiar as it does. You see, I've done this all before. It's nothing new.

Reaching his hand up, he grabs my throat and squeezes. "Butterfly, don't make me hurt you already."

His voice is low and threatening, "Get in the fucking cage."

He releases my throat, and I gasp for air as he points at the open door, and I walk around and crawl into the cage. I expect him to leave but he doesn't, instead he takes a seat in the brown leather chair down here in his basement, the only furniture aside from my new metal home.

"If you need water, it's there in the corner."

I glance to my left where he was pointing and spot the water bottle, like you'd give a rabbit or a gerbil, and scrunch up my nose. "Gee, thanks."

The corners of his mouth turn up into an amused smirk. "You're welcome, Butterfly."

"I hate you," I bite like an angry teenager.

Leaning back in his chair, he grins. "Good. I'd be worried if you didn't, because I'm going to give you every reason to."

I sit on the cold metal with my knees drawn up, trying to hide my body from him.

"What did I do to you? I didn't even get on your property."

Reaching behind him, he grabs the back of his shirt and whips it over his head, revealing a heavily tattooed and muscular body that

I'm going to pretend not to notice. This asshole does not get to know how hot he is. Yet, somehow, he does. He sits on that damn chair, with dark hair that has just enough light to make it look like he's been kissed by the sun, when I'm pretty sure evil like this lurks in the shadows of a cold, dark night. His hazel eyes focus in on me like he can get me to spill everything with only a glare.

"Do you think someone else owns the wall you were hanging from, Butterfly?"

His gaze travels my body and I know, as hard as I try, he can still see parts of me I don't want him to, but I'm doing the best I can, considering I'm naked.

I shrug my shoulders. "I don't know you. I think I was at the wrong house. Please, don't do this."

He chuckles loudly in response. "I believe you don't know who I am. If you did, I wouldn't be looking at fear, instead it would be sheer terror."

I roll my eyes at him, because he acts like he's important and he's not. He's like Manny, only hotter. A hot thug, but a thug all the same.

"Alright, I'll bite. Who are you?"

He crosses one leg over the other, as he runs his thumb over his bottom lip. "You first, Butterfly."

"Athena."

With a nod, he grins. "Luca Bonetti, but everyone calls me Bones."

He leans forward and places his elbows on his knees as he stares at me. "Are you comfortable in there?"

I've been used by men my entire life. There have been many times I have had the urge to punch one in the face, but never more than right now.

"Are you always this annoying? No, I'm not comfortable. I'm sitting naked on cold metal. It's not even a flat surface. Fucking wire is digging into my skin, asshole."

12

He shakes his head at me with disgust. "Oh Butterfly. I told you not to call me that. I'm trying to be a nice guy, offering you the opportunity to earn a little time outside of your cage. But now I don't think I can, because rewarding your bad behavior will only encourage it."

"I'm sorry."

I'm a liar. I'm not sorry, but I want out of this damn metal cage. I'll play whatever game I have to play to make that happen.

He sits there with his gorgeous body in that chair, and he better keep me in here because if I have the chance, I'll stab him.

"Beg, Butterfly."

As long as I'm in this metal cage, I'll never get away from him. I sit, staring at him as I weigh my options, which are not exactly many.

I exhale a long, drawn-out sigh as bile rises in my throat. "Please. I'll do anything."

His eyes darken, with his gaze locked on my face. "You're so beautiful when you beg, but I think you're a fucking liar, Butterfly. I don't believe you'll do anything."

I have no idea what he wants from me. He said he had no intention of fucking me, yet I'm naked, which certainly suggests otherwise.

"If you let me out of this cage, I'll do anything. Whatever you want to do to me, I'll let you."

Bones chuckles obnoxiously. "You think I want your pussy? No, you can keep that, Butterfly. I have no interest in fucking you. I want to know why you were trying to get onto my property."

I raise an eyebrow in surprise because, in my experience, all the evil men in my life have wanted to have sex with me. However, I say, "If you release me from this cage and let me put on some clothes, I will tell you anything you want to know."

He drags his hand down his clean-shaven face like he's considering it. "Alright, you can put my t-shirt on, since yours is shredded, but no pants and no panties."

"Why?"

He chuckles softly again, and every time he does that, it makes me want to stab him repeatedly. "I like your discomfort, Butterfly. Your tears are beautiful, and I can't wait for more of them. That's the deal. Take it or leave it. You can cover your pretty tits, but that's it."

"Fine, a-"

Bones arches an eyebrow. "Careful, Butterfly. Finish that sentence and find out what happens."

Rising from the chair, he comes around and opens the cage, and I crawl out and take the t-shirt from his hand. "You should know, I'm not afraid of you. None of this is new for me. I've been used and abused by evil men my entire life."

He stares at me curiously. "And they didn't break your spirit? Impressive, but I'm not them and I will."

I rise to my full height, and he grips my chin. Tilting my head back, he promises, "When you die, you'll be a broken mess. It's what I do best. I destroy pretty things."

Bones grins with a satisfied expression, as he releases me and points to the chair he vacated. "Sit."

I take a seat and he towers over me with a glare. "I kept my word. Now it's your turn."

"It's a long story, but my boyfriend wanted me to steal your car."

He tilts his head curiously. "Boyfriend?"

I nod. "Kind of."

Bones folds his arms over his chest. "We'll circle back to 'kind of'. What car were you to steal? I have many."

"A red Lamborghini."

He stares at me with a shocked expression. "My favorite." Bones shakes his head with disgust. "You never would have gotten

14

anywhere near my baby. Did he tell you who you were stealing from, little thief?"

I sit on the chair with my hands knotted, twisting my fingers. It's a nervous habit I've had since I was a child. While I've had men hurt me all my life, there's something about him that tells me he's more dangerous than the others. And it's not the cage. It's the way he carries himself that makes me believe that hurting me wouldn't be hard, and he'd enjoy it.

"No. He gave me the address. He makes me steal things for him and then he sells them."

Bones rubs his thumb over his bottom lip. "You don't strike me as a stupid girl, but this suggests otherwise. There is only one way stealing from the mafia ends, Butterfly. You will be no different."

Mafia? Did he say mafia?

I swallow hard. "I'm sorry." But I know that won't make any difference to him. My only chance to live through this will be to run if I get the opportunity. I know enough about mafia men to know there will be no forgiveness. It doesn't matter how many times I apologize. It won't matter to him that I didn't really have a choice. The only thing I can hope for is a quick death, and somehow I don't think that's part of his plan.

"Name," he growls.

"What?"

He grabs the arms of the chair on either side and leans down, placing his face an inch from mine. "The boyfriend's name. Do not fucking lie to me, either. There is nothing you can do to save him," he says through angry clenched teeth.

"Manny."

I take a deep breath and exhale slowly. "Manuel Ortiz."

He nods as his phone rings and he answers it, keeping his eyes on me the entire time he's talking to someone.

After he hangs up, I notice how different he looks. Concerned. Like a human with emotions. It's not there long before he hides it all away.

"Gotta go, Butterfly. Back in your cage."

I go to argue that he promised me time out of the metal hell, but decide against it because I think I've agitated him enough. Maybe I can buy time and escape before he kills me. Doubtful, but it's the only hope I have.

Chapter Five

Bones

I stare at my father in utter disbelief. The same man who has always been the most powerful man I've known. The strongest.

"What?" I ask, because his words make no sense to me.

"God damn it, Luca. You heard me."

He's right. I heard the words, but they must be wrong.

"We'll get a second opinion, *Padre*. You don't have cancer. There must be a mistake."

My father is old school, and in our world men are not to show feelings. We are allowed to be sad, but it is never visible. Even though his words are gutting me, I give him what he expects. The mask that says I am as emotionless as he wants you to believe he is.

He flashes me a forlorn look, before reverting to his usual impassive one. "There has already been a second opinion, *figlio*, and a third. Even a fourth."

I run a hand through my hair and take a good long look at him, take in all his features. Why had I not noticed this before? The dark circles under his eyes, the tired look of his gray gaze, the weight loss. Have I really been so preoccupied with my side businesses I've missed it all along? I know my father well. If he brought me in to tell me he has cancer, it's because they are out of options.

"How long?"

He shrugs. "Four to six months."

The sadness nearly consumes me, as the memories of this office assault me. I was only a six-year-old boy when my dad built this office. I remember spinning in his black chair that seemed so much bigger back then. He had the same pictures he does today hanging on the wall. A large one with my mother, my father, and me and my brothers. My sister wasn't born yet, so she's the only one missing.

Dad always said it was his favorite, because my mom's smile touches your heart. The black file cabinet, which I have access to now, was a forbidden place for me back then. And the curiosity ended with a belt to my ass more than once.

I lean back in my black leather chair on the other side of his 'U' shaped Italian marble desk and clench my fists. "Why are you telling me now?" I bite, because I'm pissed that he's waited until he's dying to let me in on our future. If my father is gone, it affects all of us. If he dies and no one is in charge, our entire family is at risk. We'll become easy targets.

Technically, as the oldest of my brothers, Psycho would be the one to take over, but that would be a dangerous decision. We don't call Massimo 'Psycho' for no reason, and my father knows this. Hell, everybody does. With him calling the shots, we'd have a mob war on our hands in no time.

He lights a cigar, and I open my mouth to tell him he shouldn't be smoking but decide against it, because he's a dying man. He should indulge in whatever he chooses to.

Puffing out a cloud of smoke, he says, "I am prepared to make you head of the family."

I arch an eyebrow with obvious interest as he continues, "With a few stipulations."

Attempting to appear like I'm calm and collected, I cross my left leg over my right. "And what exactly are your stipulations, *Padre?*"

He takes another puff on his cigar and exhales slowly.

"You must take a wife. It's time to settle down."

I chuckle loudly. "You are kidding, right? This has to be a joke. I have never wanted a wife."

He takes a gulp of his whiskey sitting to the right of him. "No, but you want to be the head of this family. Has that changed, *figlio?*"

Shaking my head, I admit, "No, that hasn't changed. But *Padre*, a wife? I don't even have girlfriends."

He chuckles quietly before he coughs loudly. "You like fucking, yes?"

I nod slightly, because everybody knows that not so hidden fact about me.

"Find yourself a wife you'll enjoy fucking for the rest of your life. If I die before you've become a married man, other arrangements will be made."

"Is that all?" I ask, knowing I could argue with him, but it will change nothing. Once my father has made his mind up about something, it's final.

He nods slowly. "Yes, I look forward to meeting your future wife. You've never let me down, Luca. I don't expect you to now."

Rising from the chair, I walk to the door and I pause. "Father."

My voice comes out embarrassingly thick with emotion and, of course, he doesn't miss it.

"I know, Luca. Me too. I'm proud to call you my son. Go find her."

I sigh audibly as I walk through the door and out to my car. This is impossible.

I, Luca 'Bones' Bonetti, certified playboy, am to take a wife. That's the definition of insanity right there. And where am I supposed to find a wife?

Finding a woman to fuck is easy, but meeting one that I could stand to have around for a year, let alone the rest of my life? Fuck. This is the worst fucking day ever. My father is dying, and I have to get hitched. If I thought I could talk sense into him, I'd do it. Rule number one in our family; what the old man says, goes. At home and in business. The moral of this story is I am literally fucked. Of course, I have my pretty little Butterfly, but marrying her would definitely ruin my plans for ending her life. Since the moment I pulled her from the barbed wire, I've been fascinated with breaking her, until she begs me to take her life from her. Pleading for relief. And I want that. But do I want to be the head of this family more?

19

I have four brothers and every one of them is an asshole, not
unlike myself. Three of us work for my father, and want to be the
head of the family when he steps down. I guess I know he won't be
stepping down. It'll be his death that forces him out. Kage, Psycho,
and I all want the position. I know that without asking any of them.
But Reaper hasn't worked in the business for a long time. Not
because he can't handle the bloodshed.

All he wants is bloodshed.

My youngest brother is a goddamn serial killer, and can't stay
focused on getting anything else done. My father pushed him out of
the family business years ago. All four of us share dear old dad's
penchant for violence, but none of us more than him. Which is
exactly what brings me to a graveyard at two in the morning. Not
just any graveyard, our family cemetery. My little brother is quite
skilled at ending a life, but disposing of bodies, not so much.

Our family is all buried here, going back for hundreds of years.
There are rows upon rows of headstones. They are all gray, but the
writing varies by the generation. I've always found it fascinating.
The ones that have been buried the longest have things written in
Italian. The entire cemetery is surrounded by a tall black gate. That
wasn't always the case, but it had to be installed after some creepy
ass kids decided drinking on a mafia cemetery ground was a good
idea. It wasn't. We didn't kill them, although some families would
have. I chuckle to myself at the memory, because we did scare the
fuck out of them.

My youngest brother has hair slightly darker than my dirty blonde
shade. The women all seem to love his hazel eyes, which can either
appear charming or threatening depending on his mood. All of my
brothers are fit, like myself, because physical fitness was instilled in
us at an early age. I approach Reaper as he stands, looking down at a

pretty blonde woman. Well, I'm sure she was pretty when she was alive. She has a lovely golden shade to her hair, and her open eyes are a dark blue, like the ocean, although slightly glazed over now. Her skin is pale, telling me without checking her pulse that she's likely dead.

"What the fuck?"

He doesn't take his eyes off her. "Isn't she pretty? I think I want to keep her eyes. That's not weird, right?"

"Jesus Christ. You're the one we should call Psycho. Yeah, it's a little fucking weird, man."

I don't bother asking why he kills anymore, because we all know he does it for the thrill. This isn't new. I've known this for a long time. Wanting to keep her eyes, though? That's new, and creepy as fuck. My brother may be the black sheep of the family, but not in the traditional sense. He is odd, but we accept him as he is. I guess we're all fucked up that way, because most family members would not love a serial killer. And if he ever gets busted, he won't do a second of time, because we won't allow it. Right or wrong, family sticks together.

"Look, if you're going to kill people, you need to learn to dispose of the bodies. You can't be calling me at all hours of the damn night for help."

He nods slowly. "I know."

I lean up against a gravestone. "Alright, you need to figure out a way to ditch the bodies, but make sure they won't be found until the DNA has degraded enough that there's no evidence. Or better yet, destroy the evidence."

He scratches his dark hair. "What if I buy a farm?"

I'm really trying to keep up with my kid brother, but I'm too tired for this shit. And I have work of my own to do.

"Reaper, can we focus? I don't care if you buy a farm, but you need to deal with dead girl first."

He grins with a sneer. "I've done some research. A pig can eat a two hundred pound human in eight minutes."

My brother looks so proud of himself as I shake my head at him. "Is that so, Reaper? Well, you've got it all figured out then, don't you?"

He's an idiot. While he may have researched this topic, he hasn't considered everything.

"Do you know they can't digest teeth? They leave them behind. Do you know what they use teeth for, Reaper?"

Arching his eyebrow, it's clear he realizes his mistake, and I nod. "That's right, brother. DNA. Evidence. If anybody ever looks on your hypothetical farm, they'll find DNA evidence proving that you knew the dead girl."

Living dead girl blinks and jumps to her feet with a shriek. I slide to the ground and get comfortable against Aunt Eva's headstone, because clearly it's going to be a long night. I could save the girl if I wanted to, but I'm not the hero, and I'm not in the business of saving lives.

Reaper chases after the girl, who disappeared into the trees from my view, as my mind bounces between my father's devastating news and my Butterfly. I'm close with my dad. I always have been, and I can't imagine a day where he's no longer here. We all know this is the circle of life. Everybody is born and everybody dies. There are no exceptions. The possibility of taking over for him is bittersweet. I always imagined he'd retire and be around to help me, offer guidance. And his ludicrous demand for me to get married adds an extra layer of insanity. I don't know anything about being a husband, although I assume it's a lot like managing the men I do now. Maybe this will work. I'll order her to do things, and she'll do them because she's so grateful to be alive.

After waiting for well over an hour, my brother comes back, staring at me with absolute confusion. He runs a hand through his hair. "She got away. They never escape."

I chuckle because he looks like a pathetic fucking puppy. "You let her get away?"

He shakes his head. "I know where she lives. She'll never get away from me. All she did was make the game worth playing."

"So what's the plan then, little brother?"

Reaper shrugs with a sardonic grin. "I'll find her and keep her for a while once she finally begins to relax, and thinks I forgot about her. Then I'll kill her. And I'll take her eyeballs. I want her to always be able to look at me. Even in death."

Climbing off the ground, I say, "Gotta go, Reaper. I have a Butterfly waiting for me." I don't tell him about our father, because the others will be notified when he wants them to be. Not a second before.

"Thanks, Bones."

I shake my head at him and narrow my gaze. "I mean it. Figure out how you're going to handle dead bodies, or stop fucking making them dead. I don't have time for this shit. Oh, and good luck with living dead girl."

My little brother isn't a bad guy. In fact, he might have the biggest heart out of all of us. It's just hidden. He made his first kill when he was nine years old, and I think it altered something in his brain. Reaper has never gotten past the thrill of the kill. It's exhilarating. If you've never taken a life, you wouldn't understand. It's like a surge of electricity coursing through your blood. Watching the light fade from someone's eyes is exciting. I don't care who you are. We are all murderous psychos. The difference is that Reaper is addicted to the kill. I don't imagine anything will ever dull his need for ending lives. It's who he is now. We all have our own thing we're known for. I break bones, he kills people, and Kage, well, he rather enjoys making his victims go crazy by being kept in a cage, before he ends their lives. Psycho, like Reaper, is a breed all his own. He doesn't have a specific way of killing people. He will simply make sure it's painful, and involves a lot of blood.

23

Chapter Six

ATHENA

I've been sitting in this cage for what feels like days. Luckily, he didn't take his shirt back, so I've been able to avoid the metal digging into my flesh like it was before, but I'm still miserable. Only a monster would keep a woman caged like a goddamn animal. Seriously. I'm not drinking from that damn bottle. I will dehydrate before I drink from it. I did take a look to see if I could remove it, but it's impossible. There's an opening at the top where he must pour the water in, but there's no way to remove it. I suspect it's never cleaned, which only makes it more disgusting. I glance around my surroundings, as I wonder how many people have died here. It doesn't smell like death or anything, but I have noticed the drain directly under where I sit. Is that for the blood? Urine? Am I going to die in here while he watches my life force literally go down the drain? The worst part of being locked in here, is the hours I have to consider every scenario of what he might plan to do to me. None of them are good. Each one ends the same, with my death.

I turn my head to the sound of footsteps and notice Bones walking down the steps. He's whistling, like only a psychopath would. I watch him cautiously as he stops in front of me, and stares at me through the wire. "I have good news for you, Butterfly."

He opens the door to the cage. "Come on out."

I don't move because surely this must be a trick. Instead, I scoot to the back of the cage, trying to keep my distance from him. Tilting his head, he narrows his gaze at me, and speaks in an even yet threatening tone.

"Butterfly. I will not repeat myself again. Come out now, or I'll come in and drag you out by your hair."

Like last time, he points to the chair once I crawl out. I take a seat in the chair and he gazes at me. "We're getting married."

Naturally, I laugh loudly, because of course I think he's joking. The scowl on his face quickly tells me otherwise.

"Are you crazy?"

Bones narrows his eyes at me, and while I don't know him well, I quickly figure out this was not the response he was expecting. He clenches his jaw and tightens his fists, and I decide I better attempt to calm him down quickly. I have a feeling Bones is the type of man that goes from zero to sixty in the blink of an eye.

"Why are you suddenly suggesting we get married?"

His eyes darken once again as he growls, "It wasn't a fucking suggestion. It was a demand. I need a wife to fulfill my father's obligation to become head of the family. And you want to live. It's the perfect solution."

I shake my head because he really is insane.

"I'm not marrying you, Bones. That's crazy. Why would I marry the man keeping me in a cage?"

I wouldn't. There's no way. This man is not the person I want to be tied to for the rest of my life. Terrible men are not new to me, but I think Bones is next level.

"Would you rather die?"

I shrug. "I guess so, because I'm not marrying you."

He wraps his hand around my throat and squeezes. I can't breathe. Grabbing his hand, I try to pull it away, but he's freakishly strong.

"Maybe you are stupid. Do you know what I'm offering you? Most women would give anything to be in your shoes. I would take care of you. There's nothing you would want for. You'd be the most powerful woman in my world. And you choose death? So be it, Butterfly."

He releases me, and I cough hard. For the life of me, I can't catch my breath. He scowls at me. "I'll be right back. I have a parting gift for you, and then I'll give you what you want."

Chewing on my nails that have little left, I pace back and forth, as I begin to panic before he even leaves the basement. Did I just tell him to kill me? *He's going to, Athena. You're so stupid.* Maybe he'll be nice and make it quick, but I doubt that will be the case.

I watch him go up the stairs and wait for whatever he was talking about. Within minutes, he tosses Manny down the stairs. "Ten minutes, lovers. Then it's over for both of you."

If I thought Bones looked angry with me, it's possible Manny is even more furious. His dark brown eyes narrow on me as he climbs to his feet. With a sinister grin, he growls, "Princess."

I jump up from the chair and move to the other side of the basement. I know I'm going to die today, but I don't want it to be Manny that kills me. He's tortured me for a year. I don't want to give him the satisfaction.

BONES

I climb up the stairs with a smile on my face. Sweet little Athena has no clue what she has done. Did I want to marry her? Fuck no. I don't want to marry anyone, but I have to. The second she refused to marry me, it became an instant need. An obsession. She will marry me. I guarantee, with what I have planned, she'll give in quickly. I've let her think she has ten minutes with her so-called boyfriend, and that once her time is up, I'll kill them both. I'm curious about their relationship, so I head straight to my office so I can observe them. Will he tell her he loves her? Hold her? Promise everything will be okay? He's a low level criminal. It didn't take my guys long to figure out this is what he does. Manuel Ortiz targets vulnerable women and gets them to do all the heavy work, and he takes the easy paycheck. Men like him are only capable of loving themselves. I would know something about that. I'm far more powerful than her little boyfriend, but we have one thing in common. We use women. My beautiful Butterfly is no different.

Walking up my black wrought iron spiral staircase, I make my first left down the hall to my office as I feel a pang in my chest. My father bought me this house when I turned twenty-one and took an active role in the business. When he bought it, the built-in Cherrywood desk was already here. As were the multiple black filing cabinets. But the built-in library was my addition. I don't have a ton of time to read these days, but I enjoy it on occasion. Knowing he'll be gone in a matter of months is simply unbelievable. When I turn on my camera for the basement, I'm snapped back into my current reality.

I'm not a good guy. I'll never be called anybody's hero. I will end a woman's life if there's need, but I see red when I watch Manny attacking my Butterfly. My future wife. Whether she likes it or not, she will be married to me and I'll protect her, starting right fucking now. What kind of piece of shit beats his woman? I race down the hall, and take the elevator to the basement to save time. My pretty little Butterfly is going to be terrified by what she'll be forced to watch. I know once she sees what her future husband is capable of, she won't fight me ever again.

Chapter Seven
ATHENA

Manny has me pinned to the cold concrete, his knee on the back of my neck, while he pulls on my hair as hard as he can. Even someone who thinks death might be the way out of a never-ending turmoil is terrified when faced with it. He doesn't want to hurt me this time. He wants to end me. The pain is intense, but it's the inability to get a full breath that's the worst. Tears stream down my face as I spot Bones charging down the gray basement stairs. He looks terrifying. He tilts his head slightly, a glare on his face. The dark eyes are back once again. He roars, "Get your fucking hands off my wife."

His what?

Manny releases his grip on my hair and gets off me. "Your what?"

Bones glances at me. "Come here, Butterfly."

Slowly, I climb up onto my feet and walk over to him. He places his thumb on my chin and tilts my head back, before leaning his head forward. Running his tongue from the bottom of my cheek to the top, he licks my tears. "Beautiful. From now on, you only cry for me."

He wraps his arm around my waist and pulls me into his side, as he narrows his gaze at Manny. "You assaulted my wife."

Manny stares back at him with confusion. "Your wife? How?"

Bones chuckles obnoxiously. "Not legally, yet. She will be, so as far as I'm concerned, you dared to hit my wife. That will not happen without severe consequences. Get on your fucking knees."

"I'm not-"

Glancing at Manny, I see something that looks an awful lot like fear. I've never seen him like this. His eyes dart from Bones to the stairs and back again. He's considering making a run for it, and while I don't blame him, it's useless. I have a strange feeling that nobody gets away from Bones.

"Uh uh," Bones says, "You don't want to finish that sentence. Trust me, you want to do as you're told, or shit's going to get a lot worse than I already have planned for you."

Manny must believe him because he gets on his knees as he trembles slightly. Maybe I'm a bitch, because I do enjoy the fear in his eyes.

"Apologize to my wife."

"I'm sorry," he says, but I know he doesn't mean it. There's no doubt bile is rising in his throat, as the bitterness of his words physically makes him ill. Manny is never sorry for anything he does to me. Today isn't the first time he hit me, not by a long shot. I'm positive if Bones hadn't stopped him, he would've continued until I was dead.

He runs his hand under my shirt, stroking my bare skin as he torments Manny, "Fun fact, Manuel, there are two hundred six bones in the human body."

"Please, I didn't even hurt her. She's fine. I'll go and never touch her again."

Bones turns to me. "You're mine to hurt. Any other man who even thinks of putting his hands on my wife dies."

Leaning down, he places his hands on my face on either side and stares into my eyes. "Butterfly, go sit in the chair. You're going to see firsthand how I got my nickname."

I have a feeling this is going to get violent quickly, and I need to remember all the things Manny has done to me. The countless beatings, near starvation, and constant belittling.

He leans down and kisses my cheekbone softly. "He won't hurt you again. Now, do as you're told."

This man is confusing. He's cruel, yet kissing where Manny hit me was sweet. I'm not delusional enough to believe he'll be good to me. I know better. Men like him don't treat their women with

30

respect. And I'm still not nearly as convinced as he is that we'll be getting married.

I nod slowly, and walk over to the chair and take a seat, as I watch Bones approach Manny.

"Get on your feet. Oh, and feel free to fight back."

He winks at me. "I do love a good fight. Remember that, Butterfly."

I pull on the hem of the shirt nervously as Manny shakes his head. "No. I'm not fighting you."

Bones shrugs as he reaches behind him, and pulls his shirt over his head. "It was never going to be a fair fight, anyway. Remember, two hundred six bones in the human body, and I'm going to break nearly every one of yours."

I gasp as I cover my mouth in shock. I'm not an idiot. I knew he was going to hurt him, but breaking nearly all of his bones? Can he even do that?

He glances at me with a smirk, as recognition shows on my face.

Bones. He's going to break Manny's bones. This is how he got his name.

How many times has he done this? I won't dare ask because I'm really not sure I want to know.

Calmly, he takes Manny's hand. "We'll start here, with the fingers that you thought had the right to touch my wife. There are tools to make this easier, but we'll start this way."

He stands in black shorts, with all his tattoos on display. Most of his ink is black, and his chest is ripped, but I still wonder if he can actually break his bones with his bare hands. I suppose it's possible if he's strong enough, but I've certainly never seen it done. I never even imagined it until a few minutes ago.

I don't have to wait long until Manny is screaming and wriggling his body, attempting to get away. Bones takes three of his fingers and forces them back, while Manny blurts out, "Asshole."

"Wrong thing to say. I hate that fucking word."

In a swift movement, he grabs Manny's arm and forces him onto his stomach. After he pulls his arm to his side, he squats down and places his foot on his elbow, grabs his forearm and pulls up while pressing down with his foot. When he was bending his fingers, I thought I heard cracking, but I wasn't sure. Now I know I did. Manny deserves this as much as my father would, but it's still difficult to watch.

He flips him over to his back, and Manny stares at me like I should help him. Like I could. He does exactly what he did with his forearm to his shoulder, and the man I once thought of as my boyfriend nearly convulses from the pain. His face is red, drenched in sweat, and he attempts to punch Bones, which is unsuccessful, and causes him to laugh.

"Alright, I guess we'll break those next."

He does the same thing to that arm before moving to his legs. When he squats down and places his foot on his knee and grabs his foot and pulls up with massive force, Manny yells, "Just kill me! FUCK!"

Bones glares at him. "You weren't sorry when you apologized before, but I bet you are now."

Tears stream down Manny's face, the same way mine have so many times before. Opening up to him was where I went wrong. He used my past as a weapon. Exposing myself to him showed my greatest weakness. I will never make that mistake again. As I watch Bones smashing his head into the concrete, I know I won't do that again. If I thought Manny was dangerous, Bones is even more so. I'm conflicted because it's hot in a way. This man looks good without a shirt on. And of course, saying he's protecting me is also sexy. Who doesn't want a big man that will destroy anyone who hurts her? It's my *Dexter* fantasy come to life, though he could hurt me too, or worse. It's becoming crystal clear. If he wants me to marry him, I may not have a choice. I will escape from him, I'm just not sure if it'll be before or after. I will do whatever it takes to make him believe I'm accepting my fate, but I never will. I've been in captivity for my entire life, and I refuse to end my life the same way.

Bones stands and stares at me. "Come here, Butterfly."

Rising from the chair, I nervously walk over to him, unsure of what he's going to do to me. He planned to kill me, I know that, but now that he's fixated on me becoming his wife, I don't think he's going to follow through on that threat, but still I'm unsure. He seems to go from fine to angry in a nanosecond, so I'm not stupid enough to believe he won't ever kill me. Once I make my way over to him, he says, "Take the shirt off."

I do as he told me to, and pull the t-shirt over my head as I stand in Manny's blood, with Bones staring at me with a heated expression. His eyes travel the length of my body, causing me to shiver from his gaze. I don't understand it, but it's almost as if I can feel his fingers on my skin, everywhere his eyes touch.

"On your knees."

I try to move away from the pool of blood on the floor, from my dead boyfriend's body, but he stops me. "Kneel in his blood."

Swallowing hard, I get down on my knees and Manny's wet blood touches my skin, as Bones drops his pants. "Open your mouth."

There are few things I hate more than blowjobs. I've never been a willing participant, but that doesn't matter. They never care. My time to fight will come, but this isn't it, so I part my lips. Standing in front of me, he strokes himself slowly as I gaze up at his perfect body. His scent differs from Manny's. It's not sweaty, it's more of an orange citrus smell. His cock is big and I'm afraid of his massive size, but I don't dare complain. My life has taught me that taking it is much better than the punishment that comes from refusal. After you do this enough times, it doesn't bother you as much anymore. It's routine. Men always take what they want, without considering what it does to the girl. This man is no different.

He tangles his hands in my hair and slides into my mouth. Instantly, my mouth is full of him. There's no warming up to it. One second my mouth is empty, and the next, I'm gagging on his big cock, too big. I close my eyes as he fucks my mouth, and he growls, "Eyes on me, Butterfly."

I glance up at him and he's so beautiful to look at. Even though I don't want to admit it, he's like a work of art. His strong jaw clenches as he feels the pleasure he's practically stealing from me. Yet, I don't hate it as much as I should, and normally do. He fists my hair, causing a slight sting, as he pulls out of my mouth most of the way and slams back in, making me gag a little.

"Good girl, gag on my cock. Fuck. Don't swallow."

Gripping either side of my face, he thrusts his hips forward, fucking my mouth with the occasional grunt that I'll never admit is sexy. Bones groans as he orgasms in my mouth. He pulls out with a sexy smirk that I shouldn't like.

"Show me."

I open my mouth and he nods with satisfaction. "You look beautiful with my cum in your mouth. Swallow. Every. Drop."

He pulls me to my feet and pulls me into his arms, kissing me on the top of my head. He speaks low, "I didn't know he was going to hurt you. If I did, I never would've left you alone with him. I won't make that mistake twice. Do you understand that you'll be my wife? Have you accepted it?"

"Yes," I say, while the tears drip down my cheeks. I'm not happy about it, but if I die, I don't want it to be the way Manny did. He will be my husband because I don't have a choice. However, if I get the chance, I'll stab him in the throat.

"I'm going to take you upstairs. Don't do anything stupid, and I won't keep you in the cage. I'd prefer not to have to lock up my wife, but I will."

He pulls back from our weird embrace and stares at me. "Understood?"

I sigh audibly. "Yes. I won't do anything stupid."

Bones seems satisfied with my answer, and maybe even believes it. That was his first mistake, because I am indeed waiting for the moment to try something. Hopefully end his life, before he takes mine.

Chapter Eight
ATHENA

"Follow me."

I walk behind him and he turns to me. "In front. I don't trust you."

I move in front of him. "You shouldn't."

He reaches around me and wraps his hand around my throat, and pulls my back against his front. "Careful, Butterfly. Your expert cock sucking skills won't save you. I won't kill you right now, but that doesn't mean I won't hurt you. And if you can't behave, you'll go back to the cage. Is that what you want?"

"No," I whisper when he removes his hand. He wasn't really causing me pain, but I don't have any doubt that he will. I believe every word of his warning, but if he's expecting me to obey his every command, he's going to be disappointed. No matter what anyone has ever done to me, I've never been that person, and I'm not going to start now. Of course, I do plan on not going back into the cage. I'd rather he beat me, or even break a few bones, than to go back to the metal hell.

We step into what looks like a large living room. Jesus, how much money does this guy have? The ceilings all have crown molding. I glance up at the ceiling with a gasp, as I spot the large mural that is nothing short of breathtaking. It has images of several Greek Gods and Goddesses, including Artemis, Goddess of the Hunt and Moon. The recessed lighting throughout the ceiling lights it up with such beauty. She looks fierce, holding a bow in her hand, with a full moon behind her. Turning around, I spot three large bay windows side by side. I walk further in the room to spot a fireplace. The top appears to be made of stone, but the bottom looks like marble. There's an emblem in the bottom middle portion of the stone, hand carved, three skulls, one with a crown and wings on the side.

Bones points to the spiral staircase. "Up."

I walk to the staircase, and am again astonished by the amount of money in his home. It's wrought iron, with metal flowers throughout, and dark wood covering the railing. Once we make it to the top, I gasp. The entire upstairs has the same wrought-iron railing throughout, and you can see the entire side of the house we were on, almost like a balcony in a theater. It's impressive.

"This house is amazing, Bones."

He smirks at me. "I know. If you can behave yourself, you'll get to enjoy it."

We walk down a hallway into a large bedroom, and more gorgeous decorating greets me. The ceiling is a dark blue, that seems to be mixed with a lighter blue, and more recessed lighting. There's a king-size bed with black sheets against the wall furthest from the door. There's another bay window, as well as a set of doors that appear to go to a balcony.

Bones takes my hand and pulls me into the bathroom, causing me to gasp again. My father is not poor, but I've never seen a home like this, although I wasn't allowed to travel much. I glance around the room, taking in the shower large enough for six people. It's done in earthy colors and looks like marble. There's a large jacuzzi tub across from it with four stone pillars around it, and gold taps. I wonder momentarily if the taps are actual gold, because it seems he certainly has enough money to do something so ridiculous. There's a vase of roses on each side of the steps leading up to the tub. They must be fake, because I don't think blue roses are real, but they don't look fake.

He chuckles as he turns on the shower. "Have you been living in a cave, Butterfly? You act like you've never seen a nice house before."

"Something like that."

Is he taking a shower with me? I have been fucked many times, but I've never showered with a man. It seems more intimate than we are, and it confuses me.

He smacks my naked ass. "Get in. You're wasting hot water."

I roll my eyes because he can't see me, and get in. He climbs in after me.

"Do you not have more than one shower in this mansion?"

Bones laughs lightly. "Of course I do, but you have to earn my trust."

I turn to him in the shower. "Are you afraid I'm going to kill the big bad mobster?"

He smirks at me. "No, I'm not worried about that, Butterfly. You're more likely to steal my shit. Pretty little klepto."

I glare at him as I lean my head under the spray. "I do not have an uncontrollable urge to steal things."

He turns on the shower head behind him. "Then tell me how this business arrangement with Manny happened."

I shake my head, refusing to tell him, because I am not doing what I did with Manny. There's no chance of me opening up to him so he can use my life against me. They say the definition of insanity is doing the same thing over again and expecting different results. I'm not risking myself like that again. Lesson fucking learned.

"Athena."

I glance at him, trying to ignore his Greek God body, water dripping down his skin like he's a gorgeous statue in a water fountain.

"You said I have to earn your trust. It goes the same for you. I said I'd marry you. Is that not enough?"

He shakes his head. "Not even close. I want everything, but for now, it's enough."

I pump some shampoo from the wall dispenser and wash my hair, not responding to his comment because he can want everything, but he's not getting it. I will remember who this man is. I won't let my guard down, because I've seen with my own eyes how dangerous he is. The sound of Manny's bones breaking is still echoing in my brain. I'm not sure the sound will ever fade from my memory.

The last thing I expect is for Bones to drop to his knees with a soaped up loofah and wash my legs, but that's exactly what he does. Does he do the odd sweet thing to fuck with my head?

Leaning his head down, he presses his face between my legs and inhales. When he speaks, his voice comes out gruff, "Fuck, Butterfly. This scent is intoxicating. After I marry you, I intend to eat this pussy until you're trembling for me."

Bones glances up and sees my expression and chuckles. "Please tell me I'm not marrying the one woman that doesn't like oral sex."

I shake my head. "I don't know. Manny was my first, and he didn't do that. He thought it was gross."

He rises to his feet and cups my face. "I will fucking devour your pussy. He was a boy. Soon you'll find out what it's like to be fucked by a man. You may not have wanted this, but it's your life now. And it doesn't have to be all bad."

"Will I be kept in the cage?"

He nods. "Yes, when I can't be here, unfortunately you will need to wait in the cage until I can trust you."

This is the place where hope goes to die and with one word, he destroyed every ounce I had. You can destroy someone physically or mentally. Keeping a person in the cage will take their will to live. If there's a more inhumane treatment, I don't know what it is.

Hanging my head down, my words come out in a small voice barely above a whisper. "I know attempting to steal from you was wrong, and I'm sorry. You could rape me, beat me, or break my bones. There is nothing you could ever do to me that's worse than putting me in a cage. Bones, please don't put me back in there."

Chapter Nine

BONES

I know I'm supposed to feel something when I stare at the tears rolling down her cheeks. The sadness in her expression should make me find another way. I'm as broken as the bones I shattered earlier today, because it does the opposite. It makes me fucking feral for her. I want to fuck her with the most animalistic need I've ever known, but I can't. Not yet.

My mother will ask if I'm fucking her, and I need the answer to be no. I guarantee my mom does not know that my father has insisted I take a wife. She'd never agree with it. My parents did not marry for love, and she has always been adamant that her children would never enter into an arranged marriage. This isn't exactly arranged, but she would look at it the same as if it were. I have never in my adult life lied to her, and I have no intention of starting now.

"Finish up and get dressed. I'll put clothes on the bed for you."

After drying off, I head back to the bedroom and pull on a pair of sweatpants. Can I hear her crying from the bathroom? Of course, I can. Instead of telling her that this is really all her fault, I choose to ignore it. I'm sure she knows this already. She's probably in there beating herself up, as she should be.

Athena comes out of the bathroom with a towel wrapped around her gorgeous body, as she stares at the tank top and shorts I put out for her with a glare. A furious glare. I don't mind it really because pissed off is sexy on her, even if it did catch me off guard.

"I'm not wearing some skank's clothes."

Arching an eyebrow at her, I warn, "Watch your mouth. My sister is not a skank."

Her shoulders relax, as does her face, before her expression turns to a fearful one.

"I'm sorry."

She walks over to the bed and gets dressed, first by putting the shorts on under the towel, as if I haven't already seen her naked. As if I won't be seeing her without clothing again.

"You may want to start thinking before speaking. That sharp tongue is going to get you into trouble. I'm half tempted to let you sleep in the cage tonight, instead of a nice warm bed. Is that what you prefer?"

Athena stands before me, with dried tears on her face now mixing with new ones. She looks fucking delicious in tiny black shorts, and a tight tank top that shows off her pebbled nipples. Her long wet hair hangs past her shoulders, begging for me to wrap it around my fist while I fuck her pretty cunt. Will she cry when I fuck her? Beg for me to stop? Or will she willingly give me what's mine?

I walk over to her and she backs up until she hits the wall, narrowly missing the mahogany dresser beside her. She trembles slightly, and it makes my desire for her intensify. Brushing my thumbs over her nipples, I lean down and speak into her ear. My voice is low and gravelly, likely telling her how badly I want to be inside her.

"You want me to fuck you, don't you, Butterfly?"

"No," she squeaks in a shaky voice.

I chuckle softly. "When you marry me, I'll own you, and I will take you whenever I want to."

She tries to appear brave. "I'm pretty sure it's illegal to own people in this country."

I can't help the laughter that bubbles out of me. She's so fucking cute. "Oh, trust me. I do many things that aren't legal. Owning you will only be one of many."

Wrapping my hand around her throat, I gaze at her wide eyes, that plump trembling bottom lip, and the need to taste her overwhelms me. I know I shouldn't because this is how it starts, and I'm not sure if I'll be able to stop, but she darts her tongue out and licks her lips, and I lose control. Slamming my lips to hers, I forcefully push my tongue into her mouth. I pull back to change my angle, and she bites my bottom lip so hard I taste the copper of my blood.

I stare at her while I run my tongue over the cut on my lip. "Fucking beautiful. I like it when you fight me, Butterfly. How hard will you fight for your ability to breathe?"

I'm not trying to hurt her, but I am attempting to teach her a valuable lesson.

Her eyes grow wide and teary as I squeeze my hand around her throat, cutting off her air supply. "That's right. You do nothing I don't allow you to do. Including breathing. Tomorrow you'll be my wife, and then we'll see how hard you'll really fight."

I let go of her throat, and she rubs her fingers over her skin as she coughs. "Tomorrow?"

With a smirk, I confess, "Yeah, tomorrow, because I can't wait much longer to slam into that pretty pussy."

She rolls her eyes at me. "You're a deviant. The goddamn devil."

I chuckle. "You have no idea, but you will find out. Tomorrow."

"Do you really want to fuck someone that hates you?"

Stroking my fingers down her cheek, I admit, "Yes, Butterfly, I do. The more you fight, the harder it'll make my cock. The more you cry, the more I want it. I want you to fucking bleed for me. I already know how your blood tastes. I want more."

"Fucking vampire," she grumbles.

Shaking my head, I say, "I'm tempted to shut you up by fucking your mouth again, but you need to eat. You have a big day tomorrow. Follow me."

"I'm not your goddamn pet," she blurts out.

I run a hand through my hair. "Would you like to eat, or would you like to spend the night before your wedding in the cage?"

"No," she shakes her head, "Please. Anything but that."

Obviously, I don't expect her to like the cage. No one ever does. I learned that little trick from my brother, Kage. He does it because he gets off on it. I do it out of necessity. Her reaction to it is worse than anybody I've ever seen, and it makes me curious about her past, but I don't bother asking because I know she isn't going to tell me about any of that right now. I do wonder if Manny kept her in a cage. I have figured out that he did not treat her well. Neither do I, but I won't beat her. I don't beat women. Kill them if I need to, but assaulting a woman? Especially one that's mine. That's not something I'd ever do. Keeping her bound to my bed, and using her repeatedly, is something I'll do. I have friends in the BDSM lifestyle and it's never been my thing. Somehow, I'm now seeing the draw, because my pretty little wife will look so beautiful tied up, crying while I fuck her relentlessly.

"You're ready to eat, then?"

Athena nods. "Yes."

"Good. Let's go get you food."

She stares at me. "Are you going to put a shirt on? It's a little," she waves her hand in the air, "distracting."

I chuckle. "Afraid you can't stop yourself from jumping on my dick, Butterfly?"

Her blush is instant and fucking beautiful. "No thanks. I already told you if you want to fuck me it'll need to be by force, because I'll never consent."

Grabbing her hand in mine, I chuckle lightly. "I don't need consent to take what I own, but I guarantee you, not only will you consent, you'll beg for me to fuck you."

Athena laughs, but there's no humor behind it. "Are you always completely delusional?"

I tighten my grip on her hand. "Are you always such a fucking brat?"

"Only for you, Bones," she says as we walk into the kitchen.

I point to the dining room table, telling her to sit. "I'm a lucky man then, Butterfly, because I promise I'll thoroughly enjoy spanking your ass."

"You're such an asshole," she says as she plants her pretty ass in the seat.

Arching an eyebrow, I say, "What did I tell you about calling me that?"

I move over to her as she grins. "Aww, poor Bones. Is that your trigger? You're not going to cry, are you?"

Gripping her face in my hands, I glare at her with a growl. "Fuck, Butterfly. I'm going to enjoy breaking you. And trust me, you will be broken. There's more than one way to break a person. I have shit to do tomorrow and believe me, I'm going to get off on putting you back in your cage."

Instantly, her demeanor changes. There really is no fear greater than the cage for her. And I know I'll get her to do anything I want her to, with the mere threat of it.

Letting her go, I grab a plate of food from the refrigerator for her and heat it up in the microwave. I set it in front of her, and she keeps her head hanging low with a quiet voice, "Thank you."

She picks up her fork and eats the roast my chef made yesterday. I watch her eat and attempt to ignore the satisfaction in my chest. This ridiculous fucking feeling of wanting to take care of her. It's fucking stupid, so I shove it away. There's no room for any emotional bullshit. There's no room in my life for weakness, and I simply will not allow it.

"This is good. Did you cook it?"

I laugh as I take a seat across from her. "No. I probably couldn't cook toast without burning it. My chef made it."

Glancing up at me, she giggles. "Of course you have a chef."

I nod in agreement, because there is nothing good in this life I don't have.

She smirks at me. "Although you should know, they make these things called toasters. The bread automatically pops up when it's done. No risk of burning it. You should look into them. I'm pretty sure you could afford one."

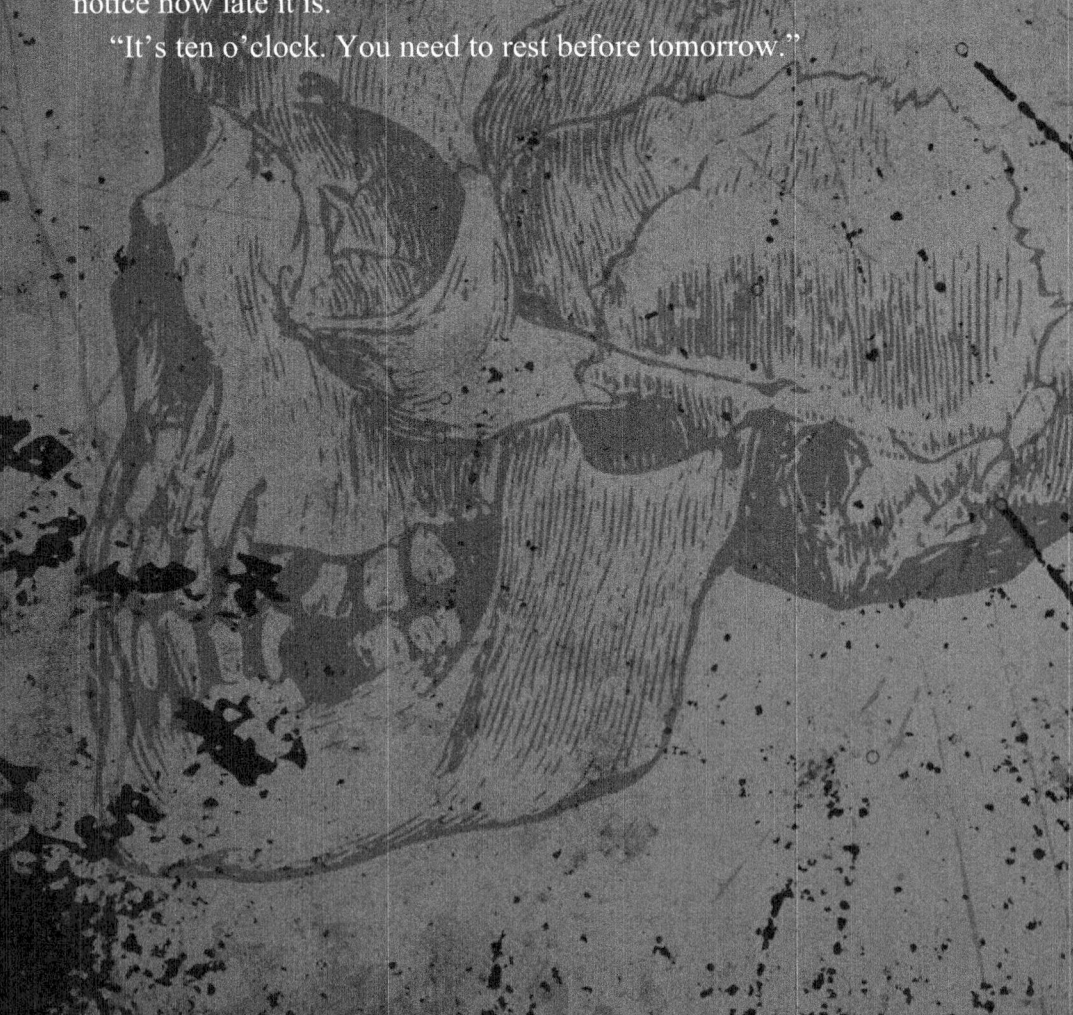

"Smartass."

Athena glances up at me, and flashes me the first genuine smile I've seen on her face. "Always."

Her eyes change when she smiles, and I've seen some truly beautiful women, but nothing like this. It reminds me of seeing the mural on my ceiling for the first time. The way the colors all come together with absolute perfection. Like the Goddess Athena, she has a strength to her I didn't expect. My future wife has vulnerabilities like any other person, but also a fight that I'll enjoy. One she'll need to survive me.

After she helps me clean up for dinner, I glance at the time and notice how late it is.

"It's ten o'clock. You need to rest before tomorrow."

Chapter Ten
Bones

"What are we doing?" She asks when I take her up to the bedroom.

I glance at her and smirk at her nervous energy. She thinks I'm going to fuck her and I plan on it, but not tonight.

"Going to bed."

Her eyes widen to the point of her looking like the most adorable cartoon character, and I chuckle. "To sleep, Butterfly."

Athena folds her arms over her chest defiantly. "You have a billion rooms in this mansion. There's no reason I should need to sleep in here."

Oh, there are many reasons I want her in my bed. I want to smell that sweet vanilla scent of her skin. Feel her soft body against mine. Listen to whatever sounds she makes in her sleep. I want it all, but I won't tell her that.

"There are not a billion rooms, Butterfly. There are eight bedrooms, but this is where you'll be sleeping, unless you prefer the comfort of your cage. I cannot trust you. Keep your friends close, keep your enemies closer."

Athena gasps loudly, almost as if she's offended. "Maybe you shouldn't marry your enemies, and you wouldn't have to worry about it."

The angry little scowl on her face makes my dick hard as a rock. It would be so easy to hold her down and shove my cock deep inside her pussy. I bet it would wipe that angry fucking look from her face.

"There are toiletries in the bathroom. Go use them, and get your ass into bed."

She stomps her feet and slams the door behind her like a little brat, which is exactly what she is. I should go in there, bend her over the sink and spank her ass, but if I do that, I'm going to fuck her. I only have so much restraint, and seeing red marks from my hand on her skin would destroy it.

Athena steps out of the bathroom and notices I've taken my pants off. She stares at my cock with surprise. "No," she breathes.

Chuckling, I say, "Yes. I always sleep naked, and you will too once we're married."

I get into bed and pat the mattress beside me. "Come on."

She grumbles to herself, "How is this my life?"

Walking over to the bed, she gets in beside me and instantly turns away from me, which is just fine. It's her ass I want, anyway.

Brushing her hair from her neck, I press my nose against her skin and inhale. Fuck. She smells amazing. Feminine. I wrap my arm around her waist, and run my fingers under her shirt so I can touch her skin.

"Bones," she whimpers as she wiggles her ass, trying to get away from my hard cock, but accomplishes just the opposite.

Her skin is like silk under my fingertips, and I don't miss the way her breathing gets heavier. She may never admit it, but she likes my touch and wants more.

"Can you not find a woman to marry you that actually likes you?"

I chuckle against her skin. "It's doubtful, Butterfly. This might surprise you, but I'm not a likable person to most people."

She giggles softly, and it only makes my cock harder. "No, Bones. It does not surprise me."

She whimpers, "No," as I kiss her neck, but the way she presses against my cock tells me her no means yes.

"You're killing me, Athena."

She groans softly. "I'd like to kill you."

Her words make me smile, because I know for a fact the first time I take her, she's going to fight me. Hell, maybe I'll give her a knife while I do it.

48

I can't help myself. Reaching into her shorts, I cup her pussy. "You're wet, Butterfly. Drenched. Tell me again you don't want me to touch you."

She doesn't say the words I know she wants to say. As I rub her clit, she moans, "Oh my God."

Her response to the slightest touch has me curious about her experience.

"Did he make you come?"

"What?" she asks, sounding surprised by my question.

I pinch her clit, causing her to yelp. "Did Manny make you come?"

"I don't know," she admits, causing me to smile behind her ear.

"You will know when you come for me, Butterfly."

That fucker never gave her an orgasm. There's no way you can not know. I rub her clit in slow circles, and her breathing becomes shallow.

"Oh my God," she moans.

"There's no God here, Butterfly. You'll say my name when you come."

Athena pushes her pussy against my hand like she needs a firmer touch, so I give it to her. Increasing my speed, I rub her swollen clit harder and she tosses her head back, and I remind her, "When you come, I want to hear my name."

A breathy scream comes out of her, stunning me, "Luca!"

Her body trembles against mine as I try to make sense of what just happened. I meant for her to say Bones. I've been known by that nickname since I was twelve years old. Nobody calls me Luca except for my parents. Not my siblings. No one.

"What did you call me?"

She giggles as I remove my hand from her shorts. "Luca," she says like it's obvious, "That is your name, right?"

I release a sigh. "Yeah, it is. Go to sleep, Butterfly."

49

My biggest issue isn't that she used my first name, it's the way it made me feel something. I don't like it, and I'm going to need to make that a rule.

Chapter Eleven
ATHENA

I didn't sleep well last night, worse than in a cage. How can you possibly get good rest with a monster holding you tightly? His arms were wrapped around me like a damn boa constrictor threatening to squeeze the life out of me. I laid there awake most of the night, only falling into a light sleep occasionally. He slept just fine, while his enormous hard cock poked into my ass, reminding me of what he plans to do to me tonight. Things I don't want, regardless of how hot he is. If I'm honest with myself, it's not him having sex with me that bothers me. It's that I know when he leaves to do whatever he needs to, I'll be in the cage again. While I don't trust him, I wasn't worried that he'd do something to me in the middle of the night. It was my fear of being put back in today. As if not sleeping would prevent it. I waited for him to loosen his grip and roll over, so I might find a way out of this hell, but he never did.

He clears his throat as I finish my last bite of breakfast, and takes my plate and cleans it off before putting it in the dishwasher.

"Butterfly, please don't fight me. I don't want to hurt you. Not today."

I laugh bitterly at him for acting like this day means anything to him.

"If you haven't changed your mind, I'll be your wife later today. Bones, this isn't how you start married life. If you do this, I'll never forgive you."

He smirks at me like my misery entertains him greatly. "I know you won't. I don't need your forgiveness, Butterfly. That's what my priest is for. Let's go."

I rise from my seat and follow him back to hell. My heart pounds furiously as we walk down the gray stairs, and I spot the cage.

"Bones, please. Can't you just lock me in the basement and not put me in there? I'm begging you. I'll do anything."

Tears spring to my eyes as he turns to me. "Fuck, you really are beautiful. I could do exactly that, Butterfly, but this will help teach you to obey. This is part of breaking you."

I drop to my knees, unsure of what else to do. "Bones, I swear, I'll be obedient."

He chuckles as he reaches down and strokes my hair. "I'm not sure you know the meaning of the word. Get in the cage, Athena. I won't tell you again."

Bones walks over and opens the cage door, and of course, there's nothing I can do, so I crawl inside. He locks the cage and watches me, the way you would any trapped animal.

"This will be your only warning. My mother will be at our wedding later today. If you do anything to upset her, I promise you, you'll live in this cage for the rest of your days. She believes this is consensual, that we're in love, and she's going to keep believing that. Do you understand?"

"Yes," I whimper as the sobs come unwillingly.

"Don't cry too much. It'll make your eyes puffy, creating more work for the poor lady doing your makeup."

I hope I get the opportunity to stab this asshole that is clearly more concerned over a woman's workload than his future wife's wellbeing. I didn't even blame him when he put me in a cage after finding me trying to get onto his property, but now; planning to marry me and still doing it tells me the horrible man he is. Men don't do this to their wives. Or future wives. I have no doubt, he'll be as terrible to me as Manny was, or worse.

BONES

I could've stood staring at her all fucking day. She looked like the definition of destruction, but no less beautiful. Maybe more than she had been last night. I don't have any intention of keeping her in the cage once it's unnecessary. She doesn't know that, and right now she doesn't need to. Honestly, I didn't want to leave her at all, but I have businesses to pop into. It's important they see the boss, as a reminder of who they will deal with if they fuck around or fuck up.

I'm standing in my underground casino beside Domenic De Luca while he plays a hand of poker, as I watch her on my phone every few minutes. He laughs after I tell him I'm getting married.

"Bones the Unmarriable?"

I arch a brow at him. "My father insists I take a wife, so here I am."

"Arranged then?"

Shaking my head, I admit, "No. He hasn't met her yet."

He chuckles lightly as he stares at his poker hand. "Does she want this?"

"Not exactly. Right now she's in a cage."

Domenic smirks at me before saying, "Does she own you yet?"

I flash him an 'are you fucking crazy' look, and he chuckles loudly. "Just wait, Bones. Your life is about to be bulldozed in the best fucking way."

I don't bother telling him how wrong he is, because I spot something on my phone I've seen before. Something I don't like. Athena backs up in the cage, sobbing and yelling. I turn on my earpiece so I can listen privately. "Please, daddy, don't. It hurts."

Instantly, I see fucking red, and know I have to get her out. I nod to Domenic. "I have to go. Try not to win too much of my money."

I nearly run out of the casino, which is really a mansion, and go to the valet and demand my car immediately. Luckily for Ryan, our newest valet, he's quick with it, and I climb in and speed off to get to Athena.

The entire drive home, I hear her crying in my mind. And why the hell it bothers me like it does, I don't fucking understand. She was huddled in the corner and fear isn't new to me, but this was different. It was pure terror.

Racing into the house, I fly down the basement stairs to find her still sobbing in the corner, so I quickly open the cage, but she doesn't respond to me.

"Butterfly."

She glances at me and covers her mouth, a strangled sob escaping, and she quickly crawls to me and throws herself in my arms, causing me massive amounts of confusion. She hates me, doesn't she? Athena sobs into my chest, as I return her embrace and hold her close to me. Did her own father do this to her? I promise you, if he did, he's a dead man. Or am I wrong? Did she call Manny 'daddy'?

Athena pulls her head back as she calms herself. Her lashes flutter as she lifts her gaze to mine and she whispers, "I don't like the cage."

People call me an asshole even though it pisses me off, because it's true, I am one. Yet, I know after seeing this, the cage is no longer an option, but I will find something she doesn't like to use to punish her. I won't have a disobedient wife. In our world, it's not unknown for our women to be tortured. I've seen a woman having a flashback more than once, and I won't be the cause of it. Not for my own wife. I enjoy her tears, but this was in a way I don't like. Shit. I care. That was not part of the plan, and I'll need to be careful to not make

Domenic's prediction come true. I'll maintain complete control of her, minus the cage.

Lifting her into my arms, she wraps her arms around my neck as I walk her upstairs to my bedroom, so she can rest before tonight. After laying her on the bed, I go to walk away but she grabs my hand, pulling me to her, so I sit beside her. "Please don't put me in there anymore."

I nod. "I'm not going to. We'll figure out another way to get you to behave."

Athena smiles softly. "Thank you."

Arching an eyebrow at her, I ignore how good it feels as she strokes the skull tattoo on my hand. "Don't thank me. I don't think you'll like being chained to the wall either, but I'm guessing you've been in a cage before."

She sighs audibly. "I have. Too many times to count."

"You need to get some rest, Butterfly. My staff will be here in a few hours to help you get ready for tonight."

I watch her as she closes her eyes but continues talking. "How many people will be here?"

"Mostly family. My parents, my brothers, and my grandmother. And my sister."

Her lips part as she falls asleep, and I watch her for far longer than I'd care to admit. She sleeps in the black tank top and shorts I gave her. Long dark hair splayed around her on the pillow, and not a speck of makeup on her face, yet she somehow looks gorgeous. Maybe other women need a made up face but she's stunning as she is.

I take a seat in the chair while she sleeps, and take care of some messages I need to return because my future wife is gorgeous, but I don't trust her. There's very little doubt at some point she's going to try to get away from me.

I fight the laughter when I spot a text message from my two crazy brothers, Reaper and Psycho, with two pretty blondes. Apparently, these are their dates for the evening. At least one of them won't survive the night. Psycho is as unhinged as my other brother, but he's not nearly as predictable.

My buddy Sin texts me about an ongoing issue with an employee I've asked about. We own seven casinos in Vegas. Well, I kind of own them, but not really. On paper, Sin owns everything, but it's my money we've used to make the purchases. If they were in the Bonetti name, we'd have feds breathing down our neck pretty quickly. The employees are never allowed to gamble in our casinos, so this asshole entering one in a disguise and then, on top of it, counting cards, won't be tolerated.

After texting my brother Kage to be sure he's picking up the rings, I lean back in my chair and watch Athena sleep. She kicks the blankets off, giving me a beautiful view. My gaze travels up and down the length of her body, appreciating every curve. I'm so hard for her but the wait is almost over. *Tonight, Butterfly.*

Chapter Twelve
ATHENA

I open my eyes to Bones sitting beside me, staring at me.

"You need to take a shower, so you're ready when my staff arrives. Please remember what I said. I told you I won't use the cage, but if you upset my mother, I will have no other choice.

Behave, or there will be consequences."

He rises from the bed and leaves without another word. His threat must have been all he had to say. I fucking hate him. Okay, I don't really, but I want to. There is no part of me that wants to be married to this man. There's a knock at the door as I climb out of bed.

"Come in."

A pretty brunette comes in and closes the door behind her. She holds her finger in front of her mouth, telling me to be quiet, so I do but I'm confused, because I have no idea what's going on. She's dressed in a black and white pantsuit, with big brown eyes that stare at me.

"I'm Penelope, Bones is my brother."

Oh goody. My future sister-in-law. Maybe she's here to make sure I understand his threats.

She reaches into her expensive looking designer purse and hands me a bottle of pills.

"Tonight after the wedding, put one of these in a drink for him. It'll knock him out for at least a few hours. Take the elevator to the B2, which is the second basement, take a left, this is a dead spot for the cameras, and run for your life. Don't look back. Just get out of here."

She hands me a stack of cash. "Don't let him find this."

I stare at her in shock. "Why are you doing this? You don't know me."

Penelope shrugs as she walks to the door. "I love my brother, but I overheard him talking to my dad, and I can't let this happen. It's not right."

After she leaves, I run to the bathroom to hide the money until later. I go between putting the money in the toilet tank and under the counter. I don't have anything to put the money into to protect it from the water, so I decide to open the box of tampons, and place it in there. Hopefully, he won't look there. Opening up the pill bottle, I stuff it with toilet paper so it doesn't make noise, before placing it in the back of the drawer while I take a shower. Turning the water on, I spot the lingerie hanging from a silver hook, and realize he's even controlling what I wear underneath the dress he picked out for me.

I get undressed and step under the shower spray as I smile. I'm going to get away. His sister saved me. No more cages. He'll be my husband, because I can't knock him out with a house full of people, but that's okay. I have the cash I need, and I'll go far away. By the time he wakes up, maybe I'll no longer even be in the state. And of course, he'll look for me, which will take more time. I bet it'll be several hours before he even gets outside and begins hunting for me. Freedom. I can almost smell it. There's the tiniest part of me that thinks I'll somehow miss him, but I dismiss it. This might be my only chance, and I've got to take it.

BONES

I laugh, watching the video with my father as he puffs on a cigar.

He shakes his head. "Penelope. She always has been a little snoop."

We sit in my office, sipping on whiskey while Athena gets ready. Poor Butterfly. I know she thinks she's found a way to break free from me. Not even close. Of course, I have cameras in my bedroom, and was watching to see her behavior before our wedding. Did I know my sister was going to try some stupid shit? No, but I'm also not really surprised either.

"What are you going to do?" My father asks.

Taking a gulp of my drink, I set it down on my black desk and look at my father on the other side. "I don't know yet."

I'd really like to give Penelope a piece of my mind, but I can't, because I need her and my bride to not suspect anything. I'm not mad. On the contrary, I'm excited as fuck.

"You have three weeks until you'll take over, assuming you actually are married by the end of the night."

I nod as I flash him a serious look. "I will be."

My brothers walk into my office, and Kage tosses me two ring boxes. I open them with a slight smile.

One has a platinum wedding band for me with diamonds, but it's the other one I want to see. Opening the box, I spot her band that matches mine, and an engagement ring with a large square shaped solitaire diamond. Six carats for my naughty little Butterfly. She may not have a choice in marrying me, still I will make sure she has the best of everything in this life. My three brothers all settle on the couch together, and Psycho starts laughing like someone told a hilarious joke. Apparently one only he can hear. I raise an eyebrow. "Care to share with the class?"

He drags his hand down his face as the laughter continues. "Just never thought I'd see the day. Bones, you getting married is a joke. I guarantee you, within six months, she offs herself just to get away from you."

Kage joins him in laughter. "No. She won't do that, but she might chew her arm off to escape from the shackles."

I glare at them both as my father puffs away on his cigar. There's normally at least a little truth to jokes, and I can't help but wonder if that's how it will go down. Will she be so miserable she'll take her life? I can't be that bad. She took worse from that piece of shit, Manny. I'll never hit her.

Chapter Thirteen

ATHENA

His staff came in two hours ago and helped me into the dress he chose, as well as styling my hair and makeup. I don't understand all the fuss. It's not actually my wedding day. I'm being forced to marry him. This isn't a story with a happily ever after. Why on earth we couldn't go to a Justice of the Peace or something is beyond me. Then again, his mother apparently doesn't know what's going on. Maybe this is for her. I sit waiting for Bones to come and get me, in a white dress that is really gorgeous. It's strapless and falls just above the knee. It's not overly fancy, but it's more than I expected for a fake wedding.

I rise from my seat on the edge of the bed, when Bones walks into the room and suddenly stops. "Fuck, Butterfly. You look ravishing."

He looks handsome as hell in a black suit, showing only the tattoos on his hands. His dirty blonde hair is styled slightly to the side, and his face is clean shaven. If this weren't all forced, I'd be attracted to him. A woman would need to be blind to not see the way he's drenched in sex appeal, but I dismiss it, because I don't have time for anything other than hatred for my future husband.

"Ready?"

He smirks at me. "You aren't going to tell me I look good, Butterfly?"

Rolling my eyes, I laugh. "I don't think I need to tell you, you cocky bastard."

Reaching out his hand, I take it as he chuckles. "Always thinking about my cock, naughty girl."

"You haven't seen the outside yet. That's where we'll say our vows, but don't get any ideas."

I take in a deep breath as I tell my lie. "I won't. I promise."

We walk out a back door that leads out to the massive grassy property. There's a red carpet for the aisle, with white chairs on either side of it. At the front of it, there's a priest, and flowers on top of large white pillars on each side of him. Glancing around quickly, I spot an older man in a seat with a woman beside him, and three men that look like they could be Bones' brothers. They are all around the same height and stature, although two of them have darker hair than Bones. On the other side are two younger women, and one is Penelope, his sister.

Suddenly, the nausea hits me as he asks, "Ready to do this?"

"Bones, please don't make me do this."

He turns to me and cups my cheek. "Butterfly, I have plans for you tonight that do not involve the cage. However, if you force my hand, I will do what I need to. Would you like to get married, or go back to the basement?"

"Get married," I breathe. That was mistake number one for me, letting him know how I felt about the cage, because now it'll always be his biggest threat. He said he wouldn't put me in there again, but I know he will if it gets him what he wants. This is what manipulative assholes do. I told him before I'd never forgive him for this, and I meant it. The sad truth is, I know he doesn't care. He doesn't give a shit about me, or how I feel.

Bones wraps his arm around mine, and we begin walking down the aisle in front of the strangers.

"Isn't the music beautiful?" He asks, but I don't respond, because I can't hear anything over the ringing in my ears. Am I going to pass out? I hope not, because I'm sure I'll wake up in the cage.

Leaning down as we walk down the aisle, he whispers in my ear, "Breathe, Butterfly."

We reach the priest and he's talking, I can see his mouth moving, but I can't hear a single word. Bones reaches forward and strokes his fingers down my cheek, and I hate that it snaps me out of my panic. I hate that it provides any level of comfort for me.

"You need to say your vows, Athena."

"Repeat after me," the priest says.

Exhaling a deep breath, I do as he says.

"I take you, Luca Bonetti, to be my lawful husband, to have and to hold from this day forward, for better, for worse, for richer, for poorer, in sickness and in health, until death do us part. I will love and honor you for all the days of my life."

Bones takes my hand and places two rings on my finger. "Athena, receive this ring as a sign of my love and fidelity, in the name of the Father, and of the Son, and of the Holy Spirit."

"In so much as Luca and Athena have consented together in holy wedlock, and have witnessed the same before God and this company, having given and pledged their faith, each to the other, and having declared same by the giving and receiving of rings, I pronounce that you are husband and wife. You may kiss your bride."

I nearly choke on my saliva hearing him say we have consented to this marriage. Bones pulls me over to his family.

This is the part I haven't even thought about. If I hesitate, he does not. Bones pulls me into his arms and presses his lips to mine. Taking my face in his hands, he tilts my head and slides his tongue into my mouth. His kiss is passionate and possessive. The small crowd cheers as he slides his hand down my back and tips me back, making a show for his family. When he lifts me up and breaks our kiss, I'm slightly dazed.

"Athena, this is my mother, Lucia."

With a smile, I extend my hand to shake hers, and she raises an eyebrow. "Family does not shake hands. We are family now."

She envelops me into a warm hug, and I'm taken aback as Bones chuckles. Pulling back, she holds my hands and smiles at me affectionately. His mother has dark hair pinned into an updo, and is wearing a classy dark blue dress that falls below the knee. It's her smile that is the most striking to me; it's warm. Penelope looks more like their mother, but Bones favors his father. She lets go of my hands as the man with her clears his throat.

Bones chuckles. "This is my father, Lorenzo."

He's far less friendly than his wife, and shakes my hand with a brisk demeanor, and a nod. I guess this is where the asshole comes from. Although I guess this is what you can expect from the man that leads a mafia family.

Bones places his arm around my waist. "Butterfly, these are my brothers; Kage, Reaper, and Psycho."

I gasp at his words, because those names sound terrifying. If Bones got his nickname from his excitement of breaking bones, why did the others get theirs? Do I even want to know? He chuckles softly as he whispers in my ear, "Yes, wife, it's exactly what you think, but you're safe with me."

Safe with him. Sure, until I piss him off and end up in the cage again.

"And this is Penelope."

I shake her hand, pretending we've never met before, and she does the same.

Bones says, "I'm going to take a moment with my wife. Eat, drink, enjoy yourselves."

He pulls me to the other side of the massive yard and stares at me. "Are you planning to behave yourself, wife?"

I nod. "Yes. I'll be the perfect wife tonight. I'll make you a drink, get you food, whatever you need."

He takes a little piece of hair hanging down, framing my face. "So beautiful, Butterfly. You're mine now. I own every inch of you."

Rolling my eyes, I say, "You don't own me, Luca."

With a groan, he wraps his hand around my throat. "I will prove to you tonight, when I'm fucking every goddamn hole you have, how much I own you."

My eyes widen, and of course, his response is laughter. "Oh yes, Butterfly, even your sweet little asshole."

He moves his hand slightly, and rubs his thumb along my bottom lip. "Open and suck."

Glancing over his shoulder, I'm relieved when I don't see anybody watching us, and part my lips. He presses his thumb into my mouth, and I suck his digit as he groans.

"Good girl," he says, and I immediately hate myself for how those two words make me feel. Bones pulls his thumb out of my mouth with a grin. "I need to get my wife food. She has a long night ahead of her."

Yeah, a long night of running my ass off. This has to work, because I know it's only a matter of time until he locks me up again. And I won't live that way. In constant fear over the worst moments of my life being repeated.

We walk back over to where everyone else is, enjoying their food, and laughing like this is an actual celebration, and Bones places his arm around my waist, pulling my body close to his. Once we approach the large display of food, he puts food on a plate and hands it to me, before getting his own.

"Thank you."

He smirks at me. "I have expectations for you as my wife, but I will take care of you. You're mine, and that means you'll have every need taken care of."

I roll my eyes as I swallow a bite of food. "Except freedom, right?"

Bones grins at me. "You'll never have that. It's not what you need anyway."

Ignoring him, I take a bite of *braciole*, and join him at the table. He sits beside me instead of across from me, like I might run at any moment. He's right to fear that, but I won't do it when he's awake. I'm not that stupid.

When everybody starts to leave, I get excited, but try to act nonchalant. It's almost time. I just have to get him to turn his back, so I can put the pills in his drink. Once he's passed out, I'm gone.

Chapter Fourteen
BONES

My beautiful wife is about to find out what most people already know about me. Very little gets by me, certainly in my own damn house. I have every inch of this house covered with cameras. She's going to be very disappointed with how tonight turns out. I give her free rein so she can accomplish what she thinks she's going to.

"I'll see you in bed, Butterfly."

If she's surprised she doesn't show it, but I kiss her on the forehead and retreat to the bed, leaving enough rope for her to hang herself with.

Athena comes into the bedroom with a drink in her hand, a drugged drink no doubt, and hands it to me. "For my husband."

I sniff it. "Is it poisoned?"

She giggles uncomfortably. "Of course not. Where would I get poison?"

I'm sure if she could get her hands on it, she would have put something in my drink to kill me. There's nothing she won't do to get free. However, this is her real problem. There's nothing I won't do to keep her. The moment I decided she'd be my wife was the moment her fate was sealed.

"I'll be back, I need to get ready for bed."

I nod as she turns to go toward the bathroom, and once she closes the door, I feed most of my drink to the plant sitting on my nightstand. I'm a little pissed off that I might be killing my favorite plant, but I'll have to take my chances. I leave a bit in the glass, because I think that'd be normal. Placing the glass on the table, I get into sweatpants and climb onto the bed. I sleep naked but I don't want to be nude right now, because I know I'm going to be going after my wife. I close my eyes and wait.

I have no clue if I snore because I always sleep alone, at least until recently, so I part my lips and breathe deeply. She walks into the room. "Bones?"

Of course, I don't respond.

"Luca?"

Fuck, I love the way that sounds, but still I say nothing.

She giggles to herself. "Well, that was easy."

"Goodbye," she breathes, and I hear her footsteps getting further away. My house is huge, and under normal circumstances it might take me a while to find her, but since I know her exact route, I am able to give her a few extra moments. Let her almost taste freedom, before I bring her crashing back to reality.

After waiting for what feels like the longest ten minutes of my life, I go in search of her. Will she be shocked? Terrified? I hope she fucking cries for me, and I'm sure before this night is over, she will.

I grab my earpiece so I can talk to security. I'm moving slowly because I'm not worried about her getting off the property.

"My wife is on the run, do not approach her, but I need updates of her whereabouts," I say into my piece, and get an immediate response.

"She has just exited the elevator, Boss. She appears to be headed for the West exit."

The excitement builds inside me, feeling almost like my blood is on fire, and I guess it is, for her. I've wanted to fuck her since the moment I saw her, even when I said I wouldn't. I think I knew even then that I'd be inside her. When I fucked her mouth, it was obvious to me it would never be enough. I knew I had to have all of her. And now I will.

I follow in her tracks when my security alerts me, "She's outside, Boss. Do you still want us to stand down?"

With a grin, I say, "Yes. Let her think she's getting away from me. Once I get to her, I expect you to turn the cameras off. If you watch what's going to happen, I'll fire you and then I'll kill you."

68

"Yes, Boss."

I make my way outside, and immediately notice she left the black wrought iron gate open. She likely was concerned about making noise, and my security team hearing it.

Walking through, I grin to myself when I hear the crunching of leaves under her feet. This side of my property is covered in trees, and my eyes dart from left to right trying to find her. She's close because I can hear her heavy breathing, but I can't see her. Yet.

"Butterfly."

Her squeak of probably a mixture of surprise and fear makes my dick hard, but also alerts me she's off to the right. I move in that direction as her breathing gets heavier.

"Jesus Christ, wife. I love the sound of your fear."

"Leave me alone," she breathes, right before she takes off in a sprint.

I hear her crash to the ground followed by, "fuck," and I chuckle as I spot her getting back up and running again.

This is a far better wedding night for me than I could've ever planned. She doesn't know it but she has given me the best wedding gift. Finally, I'm close enough to smell her. The terror in her blood gives off an intoxicating scent. One I'll track like the fucking animal I am. Athena stumbles slightly, so I grab her leg and yank her to the ground with a thud, causing a delicious little whimper to escape from her lips. I cover her body with mine, wrap my hand around her throat, and growl, "Butterfly. You fucked up, baby. Now you get to see what you married."

I've got her upper body pinned to the ground while I wedge my leg between hers, forcing her to widen hers. With my free hand, I reach under her dress and rip her panties. "We could've done this gently for the first time, but you wanted to do it the hard way."

"No," she cries. Tears fall down her cheeks, nearly glistening in the moonlight. I pull myself out of my pants as she screams, "No! I'm not even on birth control."

I grin at her. "Good because if you were, you wouldn't still be taking them. If I have the first boy, he'll be first in line to inherit the business. It's important."

She bucks her hips, trying to push me off her, but it's a futile attempt. There's no stopping this.

"Is that all you care about? What if it's a girl, asshole?"

I shrug with a sadistic smile. "That's fine. We will keep trying until we have a boy."

My beautiful Butterfly reaches her hand up and yanks my fucking piercing out of my nipple, and the blood flow is immediate, as is the pain. She probably thought causing me pain like that would make me stop. Unfortunately for her, I get off on pain. As if she can read my thoughts, she whimpers helplessly.

Lining my cock up with her entrance, I slam inside her, causing her to yelp from the pain. I stare into her eyes. "I own you, Athena. This is mine. You are mine. There'll be no getting away from me. Had you actually gotten off the property, I would have burned the entire world down to find you. There's nothing and no one that can keep you from me."

Leaning my head down, I press my lips to hers, and she bites down on my lip again. Naughty little slut.

I chuckle as my blood coats her lips, and pull out of her pussy and slam back in. "Not rough enough, Butterfly?"

Moving my hand from her throat, I yank her dress down, along with her strapless bra, and reveal her tits. If she could figure out how to behave, she'd be perfect. Her hard nipples beg for attention, so I lean down and swipe my tongue across one. "I think since you pulled my piercing out, we'll get yours done."

"You cannot force me to get pierced."

I laugh at her while I fuck her harder. "You'd be amazed at what I can and will force you to do, baby. At least I won't beat you."

She glares at me. "There's worse things than physical abuse, Luca. I'd rather be beaten."

I ignore the pang in my chest, pushing out the emotions, and fuck my wife.

Athena bursts into tears, and I lick at the wetness on her cheeks. "Fuck, yes. Cry for me. So beautiful."

"I hate you," she cries out into the quiet night. And I know she does, yet I also know she's enjoying this.

"See how wet you are for me, Butterfly? Because as much as you don't want to, you're enjoying being fucked by your husband."

The glare in her eyes is instant. "I'd rather be fucked by Manny's dead cock."

I laugh loudly. "Keep telling yourself that while you come for me."

I'm aware she's trying to piss me off, and she does a little, but I won't let her ruin this moment for me. Her pussy feels like fucking heaven. Changing my angle slightly, I thrust inside her, knowing full well I'm hitting her 'G' spot, and she crumbles in ecstasy. Her entire body trembles beneath mine, her eyes wide with lust she'd prefer to keep hidden, lips parted as she moans through an orgasm. Fucking stunning.

Athena pants heavily as I continue fucking her. "Tell me again how much you hate being fucked by your husband, Butterfly."

She screams, "I hate you, and I hate my fucking body."

Shoving back into her pussy forcefully, her body moves under mine as she gasps. "Good. Tell me how much you hate me, while you come all over my cock again."

I try to hold off my own orgasm, desperately wanting her to come again, but she feels so good I'm not going to be able to stop it for long. Reaching down, I place my thumb on her clit and rub her in circles, as she cries, "No. Don't."

I smirk at her, because I know why she wants me to stop. Athena does not want this to feel good. More than anything, she wants me to be a bad fuck like her dead ex. I'm not and never will be. I may not care about many things, but I do care about giving my wife pleasure.

If she were smart she'd take what she can out of this marriage; endless amounts of money, and endless orgasms. This isn't a traditional marriage, I'll never love her, but I'll give her everything else. It doesn't have to be a miserable existence. Maybe, in time, she'll learn that.

Athena moans loudly as her pussy clenches down on my cock, making me lose all control. The pleasure travels through my entire body, my balls tighten, and I fill my wife. She could get pregnant. It's not my immediate goal, but if it happens, I'm fine with it. It will be important for her to bear my children at some point, anyway. I'd prefer to have her to myself for a while, but if she has my baby, she may give up this fight a little quicker.

Chapter Fifteen
ATHENA

He pulls out of me and pulls my dress back up. "I don't want my men looking at your tits."

"You knew, didn't you?"

Bones wraps his arms around me. "Of course I did, Butterfly. There are cameras everywhere in my house."

I glance down at his bleeding nipple and actually feel bad. "I'm sorry. I wasn't trying to cause damage. Why didn't you stop me?"

He smirks at me as he pulls me into his side, and walks me back to the house. "Pain gets me hard, Butterfly. The only thing you accomplished was making me want you more."

I sigh audibly. "I assume I'm going back in the cage?"

Bones stops momentarily, and kisses my cheek. "Not a chance. I'm nowhere near done fucking you. And I told you I won't put you back in there."

I want to believe him but I don't. It would be a mistake to begin trusting the man that forced me to marry him, and fucked me against my will outside like a damn animal. The same man who kept me in a cage. There's no coming back from this type of behavior. I now know my so-called husband is capable of just about anything.

He stops, bends down, and scoops me into his arms. "What are you doing?"

"I'm very traditional," he says with a grin, "Carrying you over the threshold."

I wrap my arms around his neck, and lay my face on his chest, so I don't fall, not because I'm obsessed with his scent. I don't know why but he smells like wood, leather, and spicy orange. Once again, I hate myself for liking it and wanting more. There is no part of him that should provide any amount of comfort to me. Clearly my lifetime of trauma is taking its toll on me.

He sets me down on the kitchen counter. "Now that we got your bad attitude taken care of, should we continue our wedding night?"

I can't stop the fit of giggles that bubble out of me. "Bad attitude? You've been holding me captive, and forced me to marry you."

Bones arches an eyebrow as he pours two glasses of champagne he had sitting on the counter, "Is it really forcing you when I gave you a choice?"

Setting the glasses down, he turns to the refrigerator and grabs strawberries, before closing the door.

"Marry you or spend the rest of my life in a cage? Is that really a choice, Bones?"

He hands me a strawberry. "Put this in your mouth. The next thing I want to hear from you is you screaming my name."

I take a bite of the fruit, but only because it looks really good. Reaching behind me, he unzips the back of my dress.

"What are you doing?"

Pulling the dress over my head, he growls, "I'm starving, Butterfly. You're going to be a good girl and feed me your cum."

Bones pushes me until I'm laying down on the counter. "Pull your bra down before I rip it off your body."

I roll my eyes. "You're an animal."

He grins proudly like it's a good thing. "Thank you. That might be the nicest thing you've ever said to me. Now spread your thighs, so I can make you see stars."

I do as he says, but I'm pretty sure I've never met a cockier person in all my life. He's so sure of his skills, and it's annoying, so I vow to myself to not have an orgasm. No matter what I do, I need to hold back, and not give him what he wants. I set the strawberry on the counter beside me as he presses his face against my pussy. "Are you going to come for me, wife?"

"No."

Bones chuckles. "We'll see, baby. Would you like to place a wager?"

"What?"

He stares between my legs like it's a beautiful work of art, which is weird, as he answers, "If you don't come, I'll let you go. Hell, I'll even give you however much money you need."

I lift my head up and stare at him in shock. "You'll just let me go?"

Am I being tricked? He forced me to marry him. Surely he's not going to let me go, but I don't have many options right now. This is the best offer I'm going to get. I wait for his response, as I try to keep my excitement in check.

He nods. "I always honor my word."

If he's willing to just let me go, I know he's very confident in his abilities, but I'm equally as confident in my need to get the hell away from him.

"What do you get if you win?"

His eyes travel the length of my body, groaning as he takes me in. "Nothing, Butterfly. I have everything I want."

He grips the inside of my thighs, as he stares at me with a heated expression, and his words could bring me to my knees, if I were standing. "Fuck, Butterfly, you're so beautiful. Sometimes when I look at you, I can barely breathe. And I wonder how could something so perfect be mine? The truth is, even if I didn't have to get married to fulfill my father's requirements, I never could have let you go. It's unfortunate for you that you got yourself caught in my web, because I already know, once I taste you, I'll never get my fill."

I swear, I could probably come from listening to those words from his deep gravelly voice, but then he swipes my clit with his tongue, and I flinch from the instant pleasure. His tongue is soft, wet, and hot, and hits me with obvious skill. He has done this before, obviously, but this isn't a chore for him; he likes it, and it shows. Bones groans as he moves his tongue along my slit, before dipping it inside me and moving it in circles. I can't fight the moan that slips from me, or the way I reach down and slide my hands into his hair, holding his head in place, as he ignites something inside me I never knew existed.

Replacing his tongue with two fingers, he fucks me slowly as he places his lips on my clit and sucks, and now I know what his comment was about seeing stars. I lose all control. There's no doubt I'm losing our bet. I grip his hair harder as my entire body shakes uncontrollably.

"Luca!"

He growls against my pussy, "Say my name again, Butterfly."

"Luca," I whisper and he groans.

"Come for me. I need more."

Moving his fingers back and forth, while he feasts on my clit, he gives me no choice. I've already lost the damn bet, so I may as well enjoy the pleasure. I had sex with Manny more times than I can count, but he never made me feel like this. The way Bones stares at my face while he devours me is intoxicating. I still hate what he has done to me, but I can't ignore the way he makes my body feel, the way he looks at me with pure desire.

Warmth spreads through my limbs, and my body shakes, while he groans against my clit. I cry out for him, as my back arches off the counter, and I scream his name. He stands to his full height. "I can't fucking take any more. I need to be inside you. Now."

Lowering his pants, he takes his cock in his hand as I watch him closely. I've never been so turned on by simply looking at a man's body. He pushes my legs back and slides inside me, before placing a hand on the counter on either side of me. Gripping his biceps, I hold on to him, while he rocks back and forth inside me. His strong muscles move under my fingertips, as he leans down and presses his lips to mine. I moan into his mouth as his tongue slides against mine, slowly, passionately, before he becomes more aggressive with both his kiss and his thrusts.

Wrapping my legs around his waist, I lose myself in Bones, and I think for a moment maybe everything will be okay. If every day is like this, I can live with it. He fucks me like I matter, like he needs me, and it's a powerful feeling. There's a danger in believing something might be good, because that's when someone can hurt you the most. Letting down the wall that protects you, can ultimately destroy you. I don't have much left to be broken. It wouldn't take much to push me over the edge.

Chapter Sixteen
Bones

She places her face in my neck, her breath soft against my skin, as I finish inside her with a grunt. Pulling out of her, I tuck myself back into my pants, and lift her into my arms to carry her to the bedroom.

My father told me to find a woman to marry that I wouldn't get tired of fucking. My Butterfly is that woman. I will never get bored with being inside her. Whether she's laughing, crying, or screaming, every second is pure bliss. Athena yawns against my chest and even that is beautiful.

I unsnap the bra that's nearly around her waist and toss it to the floor, right before placing her on the bed. She watches me with sleepy eyes, as I remove my pants and then climb in beside her. Wrapping my arms around her, she snuggles against my chest and says, "Bones?"

I kiss her on the forehead and she asks, "What's going to happen when you have to leave? If you're not going to put me in the cage, what will you do?"

This isn't something I've thought a great deal about, or I'd have an answer prepared.

"I'm not going to lie to you, Butterfly. You tried to run tonight, and that's not a risk I can take. Letting you have the run of the house while I'm gone isn't an option."

She pulls her head back and gazes at me, clearly waiting for my response, so I give her my thoughts.

"I'll have to chain you. I know you don't like the cage, although I don't understand why it upsets you like it does, but you'll need to be secured. You're too much of a flight risk."

The tears fall, and I decide I should just tell her everything, rip off the band-aid so to speak.

"I need to go to Vegas for a few days. You'll be chained, and I'll have a guard give you meals."

Athena tries to pull free from me but I don't allow it, she pounds on my chest and screams, "How can you do this to your wife?"

Deep down, I know she's right. I shouldn't fucking love seeing her this way, completely falling apart, but I do. There is no part of me that doesn't realize it's not normal to chain your wife up when you need to go on a business trip, yet she has given me no alternative. I can't trust her for an hour, let alone three days.

"I hate you," she cries.

Kissing her wet cheek, I say, "I know, Butterfly. I know. Now go to sleep."

Tightening my hold on her, she sobs into my chest, my beautiful broken wife, and eventually falls asleep. The truth is I could lock her in a room, armed with a guard outside so she couldn't leave. I'm not sure why, but I like the idea of her being chained up and waiting for me. I've always thought my two brothers were far more fucked up than I am, but I'm beginning to wonder.

Four hours of sleep is not enough, and I'm aware if I were a decent man, I'd leave her alone. Unfortunately for her, I'm not. I have to leave soon and I need to fuck her before I do. Rolling her onto her back, while she stays dead to the world, I spread her legs and kneel between them. Now that I've had her, the idea of not fucking her for two days is almost painful. Pinning her legs back, I line my cock up with her pussy and push inside her. She doesn't wake up, instead she moans in her sleep while I fuck her. Athena gives me a few more whimpers, before her lashes flutter and her eyes open. It takes her a moment before full recognition hits her. And my beautiful Butterfly is pissed. I climb over her so I can control her body, and wrap my hand around her throat while I support myself with my free hand beside her.

"Good morning. I needed to have you before I leave."

She glares at me and bites, "You mean before you chain me up like a bad dog?"

Her hands hit my chest as she attempts to push me off her, which will never work. Knowing I don't have much time, I speed up my thrusts and fuck her harder. Athena grabs my nipple she yanked my piercing from and pinches it, causing me to chuckle, because I already told her I enjoy pain.

"Say my name."

I can't help myself. My name has never sounded like it does coming from her lips.

"Bones," she says, followed by, "Or do you prefer the name I like calling you best? Asshole. In my head, that's what I always call you."

I glare at her while I squeeze her throat. "I think I've warned you about that. The plan was to make you come too, but you've lost that right."

Removing my hand from her throat, as I continue sliding in and out of her wet pussy, she coughs and gasps for air. "I fucking hate you."

With a chuckle, I say, "I know that already, but if it makes you feel better, go ahead and keep saying it."

I back up onto my knees, grip her thighs on either side, and rail her as she yelps. Since this is now only for me, I don't need to take my time, I can fuck her the way I want. Hard. I pull out most of the way and slam back inside her, with every thrust her tits bounce deliciously, and I catch her biting her lip to fight the moan threatening to escape.

"You're only punishing yourself, Athena. I'm not the one that will be sitting in the basement with sexual frustration, and not being able to do anything about it for two days."

81

I thought I had seen her angry before, but clearly I had not, as she sits up and bites my chest. Fucking bites me like a rabid dog. Her eyes are blue, but now they're darker than they've ever been before, and she bites me again. I push her back, and hold her hands down. "I don't fucking think so, Butterfly."

She continues glaring at me. "If you think you're going to fuck other women and come home and fuck me, you're mistaken."

Where the hell did that come from? Why would she think I have any intention of being with another woman? I wouldn't dream of fucking another woman when I can have her, the best pussy I've ever had.

Holding her down, I continue fucking her. "Listen to me, Butterfly. I'm not a good guy. In fact, in your mind, I'm likely among the worst. There are no other women, and there will not be any other women; I take my vows seriously. You are the only woman I will fuck. Hell, you're the only woman I want to fuck. I assure you, my dick is clean and it'll stay that way."

She turns her head, trying to shut me out, and I let go of one of her arms and force her head to turn toward me. I press my lips to hers, and she fights me before she finally gives in, and lets me kiss her. Her pussy clenches down on my cock and pulls my orgasm from me. She'll spend the next two days hating herself as much as she hates me.

"Get dressed and meet me downstairs."

I pull out of her and get off the bed, and get dressed in black dress pants and a matching button down shirt. Athena is still glaring daggers at me, but I ignore it, because I don't have time to deal with this. Certainly not when it won't change a damn thing.

After she has breakfast, I take her by the arm and pull her down to the basement. She immediately glances at the cage, and I say, "You aren't going in there."

I take her to the chains, and place her wrist in the restraint, and tears fall from her beautiful eyes. "Luca, please don't do this to me."

I continue with her other wrist, and then her ankles. "The bathroom is over there. You have enough length on the chains. My staff will bring you food and drinks."

I watch as she collapses to the floor in sobs. "Luca. Please."

Stroking her hair, I say, "I'm sorry it has to be like this, Butterfly."

What I really should say is that I'm sorry I am the way I am. She doesn't deserve this.

"I'll see you in a few days."

Leaning down, I kiss her on the top of the head and make my way to the stairs, listening to her sobbing as I close the door behind me. A gut wrenching scream tears through the quiet of my house, "LUCA!"

Although I'm tempted, I can't turn back now. She has to know I'll follow through on the things I say I'll do. If I show her weakness, she'll walk all over me. I learned this from my father. If we tell our guys if they steal that we'll do something, we have to do it, whether we want to or not. Showing weakness makes you a liability. As hard as it is to listen to her screams, that sound so much like the last time she was in the cage, I can't back down.

Chapter Seventeen
BONES

Stepping off the plane in Las Vegas, the sun is bright and nearly blinds me. I slide my aviators on and climb into the back of my car. I don't need to tell my driver where he's going because he knows, unless I say otherwise, it's straight to the casino with the current issue. Sitting back in my seat, I open up my app on my phone to check in on Athena. She sits with her back against the wall, a tray of food sits untouched, and one of my guys walks down to the basement with a dinner tray. He sets it on the floor in front of her, and she shakes her head as he walks away, and I watch as my wife kicks it across the room. She tilts her head back and looks directly at me, like she knows where the camera is, which cannot be the case, and while I can't hear her, I see her mouth my name. "Luca," she says, with desperation in her eyes as the tears fall again.

A text comes through from my head of security, interrupting my viewing.

Eduardo: *Boss, you said to let you know if there were any problems.*

Me: *What is it?*

Eduardo: *Your wife won't eat.*

Me: *I know. I saw the footage.*

Eduardo: *Do you want us to force her?*

I growl from the backseat, as my driver pulls into the casino entrance.

Me: *No. Do. Not. Fucking. Touch. My. Wife.*

Eduardo: *Of course not. I'll keep you updated.*

If anybody touches her, they are dead. I don't care who they are, or how valuable they are to me. There's nobody worth more than her. She's priceless.

Getting out of the car, I walk into the casino and go talk to my business partner, Sin. I'll view the footage before I decide how to handle the situation with one of our employees. I'm fair. My goal isn't to hurt people that don't deserve it. If I see proof for myself, then he's going to regret the day he was born.

I take a seat at Sin's desk, across from him, and he nods at me. "Bones. Good to see you."

"How's married life?"

He grins. "It's good. How are things?"

I shrug, and he spots my ring. "What the hell is that?"

With a chuckle, I say, "I got married."

Sin flashes me a confused look, and I'm not surprised. Anybody who knows me would have bet money that I'd never settle down.

"Long story, but my father is sick. This was his requirement in order for me to take over the family business."

He frowns slightly. "I'm sorry about your dad."

We have known each other since we were kids and he knows me well. It's good to be in business with someone that picks up on your cues. Picking up the remote for his security camera, he presses play, and I watch the footage on the tv mounted on the wall. I've already been informed by our experts that this person was card counting. However, if he's an employee, it escalates things. On top of that, I'm told that he's fucking one of our cashiers, and she randomly slips him cash, as well as chips. There is no getting away with that. Of course, there are cameras everywhere. On top of that, when you win money, a video is watched to be sure you actually won. And if money goes missing, there is always evidence.

He didn't attempt to conceal his identity well, so it's easy to know it was him.

"I assume he's at the warehouse?"

Sin nods. "Yes, he's ready for you."

We never physically deal with problems in the casino, because it puts Sin at risk. If the feds ever came in and searched, it would most certainly raise questions we don't want to answer. I rise from my seat and he asks, "Did she marry you willingly?"

I turn to him and tell him honestly, "Don't ask questions if you aren't prepared to hear the answer."

Holding his hands up, he says, "Fair enough."

He lives in a consensual world. Everything is safe words and bullshit. We are not the same and he knows I won't lie about it. I don't lie about anything. I live my life unapologetically. I always have and I always will.

I stand in front of my thief, and smile at the thought of how I dealt with my last thief. My pretty Butterfly. He won't be as lucky as her.

"Michael Watson, we have a bit of a problem. By we, I mean *you* have a fucking problem."

This room, which my employees call The Bone Room, is set up with everything I need. We have knives and other weapons here, but my favorite is a simple vise. There's a metal table off to the side, a rather uncomfortable gray metal folding chair in the middle of the room, with another metal table beside it with a blue vise sitting on top of it. Currently, Michael sits on the chair with an arm in each vise, ready for me, but they're open. Nobody does this other than me. I've been told that it's sick. I guess it's a family trait. Myself and my brothers all have special interests. I don't break bones for the hell of it. There's always a reason, but I can't say I hate it.

The satisfying crunch of bones. The spine chilling screams. The bone piercing through the skin. It's all fucking mesmerizing.

I wouldn't say it gets me off necessarily, but it does bring me pleasure. Every bone I have ever broken has belonged to someone that has wronged me in some way. If you hurt someone I care about, I consider it as a personal attack.

Glancing down at a trembling Michael, I smile at him. "Stealing from me sounded like a good idea?"

He sits in his dark blue work polo and khaki pants, and of course I don't miss the fact that he soils himself, as he trembles in the chair.

I shake my head at him. "This all could've been avoided, Michael. Had you not broken the rules and stolen from me, you would not be here."

"I'm sorry," he whimpers pathetically, causing me to chuckle. Of course, he's sorry, because they always are when they end up in his position.

"Let's get started then. I'll warn you, this might sting a bit."

I walk over to the table holding his right arm, and turn the handle slowly for the added suspense. He watches as the screw pushes the jaw plates closer. There's a plate on either side of his arms that will eventually crush them. This is a slow and painful way to go. Sometimes, I get bored and have to end their lives in other ways. However, I'm currently kind of pissed. He took me away from my beautiful wife and now she hates me, all because I had to come deal with his shit. There is no doubt, when I get home, I'll have to deal with her angry behavior. It's not necessarily a bad thing, but I'd much prefer to be at home and inside her, than to be dealing with this prick. The plates move closer and his breathing becomes erratic, so I stop for a moment. "Relax, Michael. It's not even doing anything yet."

The goal is most definitely not for this fucker to pass out, and not feel pain. His eyes widen when I turn the handle again, the plates less than a inch from his arm, and he cries, "I'll give you my house. Anything."

Chuckling, I tell him the truth, "If you saw my house, you'd realize how little I'm interested in your two-bedroom bungalow."

Slowly the plates begin to squeeze his forearm and he screams. I roll my eyes, because I know damn well it's not painful yet. Uncomfortable maybe, but not painful, and he is already screaming like he's in absolute agony. Punk ass bitches annoy me, so I speed things up and smile at the sound of crunching bone.

Now he really screams as he nearly convulses in the chair, and this time I don't judge him because it hurts. The chair buckles beneath him, and my guys rush over and set him right. This will happen repeatedly as he attempts to get away from the pain. It's a normal response. If you touch a hot burner on a stove, your normal response is to retract your hand without thinking about it. This is no different. Realistically, he knows there's no way to avoid this. Yet the brain will still make him try to run from it.

I move to the other arm and repeat the process, while whistling. That's a family trait. We all do it and yes, I'm aware it's probably a sign we're not okay mentally. As I feared, once the plates begin to crush his left arm, he passes out from the pain. The body is amazing in the way it attempts to protect us from more than we can handle. The brain specifically. My men are well trained, and Miguel brings over a hose and sprays him in the face with cold water. They are taught to know how to respond without me having to give orders.

He coughs as he wakes to water in his nose and mouth. I glance down at his red, sweaty face. "Good morning, sunshine. Shall we continue?"

I turn the handle as he moans curse words, and my phone rings.

Holding up my finger, I say, "One moment, please."

"What?" I answer as I walk away from sobbing Michael, so I can hear.

"Boss, we have a problem."

"What is it?"

"Your wife, sir. She got a hold of Eduardo's weapon and she's holding him at gunpoint."

I shake my head with irritation. "How did that happen?"

Glancing at Miguel, I order him, "Finish this. I need to cut my trip short."

Walking out of the building, I go straight to the car and inform my driver we're going back to the airport.

I climb into the backseat as Jimmy explains, and I pull up the video so I can see my wife for myself. "She played dead. Eduardo got closer to make sure she was okay, and she took his gun. Mrs. Bonetti says if we don't shoot her, she's going to kill him."

I sigh as we reach the tarmac. "Listen closely, Jimmy. Nobody touches my fucking wife, even if she shoots you, which she's rather unlikely to do. Touch her, and you've signed your own death warrant."

"Yes, Boss," he says and I hang up the phone. There's nothing I can do about it from here, so I need to hurry home. I don't believe she'll shoot them. Bite them, maybe, but she won't actually kill anyone. When I get home, my beautiful Butterfly is in so much trouble. This is why she was restrained, because I can't fucking trust her to behave.

Chapter Eighteen
ATHENA

I hold the gun in my hand, pointed at Luca's employee, the one that kept bringing me food I'm not going to eat.

The other one stands watching, while his buddy kneels on the floor as he was told. I'm not going to kill anyone, but I've been trying to get the other one to shoot me to save his friend. The guy standing by the door, I think his name was Jimmy, says, "Phone call, Mrs. Bonetti, I'm not coming any closer. I'll put it on speakerphone."

Mrs. Bonetti.

Those two words make me feel physically ill.

"Butterfly."

My hands shake uncontrollably. "Hang it up."

"Baby, please put the gun down. I'm afraid you're going to hurt yourself."

The pounding in my head intensifies, my arms and legs tingling as I listen to his voice. The one I never want to hear again, yet also need near me. Confusion scrambles my brain as I sob. "Hang up the fucking phone."

"Princess, open your mouth for daddy." I'm only six years old, I don't understand why, but I do as I'm told. Daddy says I'm a good girl and I always do as he says.

"Butterfly, please put the weapon down."

He snaps me back to reality, but then something keeps pulling me back to that dark place. I cannot control it.

"Princess, get in the cage."

I cry out, "Please daddy, I'll be good."

He drags me by my hair, and throws me inside the metal that's so cold and scary.

This time it's not his voice that brings me back to the here and now. It's the loud sound from the gun. I glance around, trying to figure out what happened, when the man on his knees falls to the ground and the other one shouts, "She fucking shot him!"

"Oh my God. Oh my God."

The firearm falls to the floor as I back up against the wall, and the fear swallows me whole. I hear Luca in the background, but he sounds far away.

"Pick up the gun. Get Eduardo medical attention, and don't fucking touch my wife."

Jimmy walks over and picks the gun up, and tucks it into the back of his pants, then he squats in front of me and gives me a terrifying glare. "You may be the boss's wife, but I promise you if he dies, you will not be safe."

Gritting his teeth, he continues while spit flies from his mouth, "You can cry for Luca as much as you want, but I'll kill you myself, Princess. Don't worry, you can call me daddy while I'm fucking you first. I hear that's kind of your thing."

He calls for help on his radio for his friend as he walks away from me, chuckling like a psychopath.

I cover my face as my lips tremble like I'm cold. I'm not. My eyes dart from him to the other guy as my pulse races. Suddenly, I can't catch my breath. Clenching my fists, I sit in my spot while the men get him out of here, and probably to a hospital. I can't stop thinking about what he said about me calling him daddy. That can't be a coincidence.

BONES

A five-hour flight from Las Vegas to New York has never felt longer than this one did. I don't honestly know what she was thinking. There was no part of me that thought she'd actually shoot anyone, but I was concerned she might hurt herself. Jimmy was told, in no uncertain terms, that he is to not touch her, and normally he follows orders. However, it's not lost on me that my wife shot someone that means a great deal to him. If it had been anyone other than Athena, I myself would seek vengeance. I'm more than a little anxious as I growl at my driver to drive faster. I torture myself with watching the recording from earlier, of Athena holding a gun on Eduardo. I pause the screen and stare at her beautiful face. Tears streak her cheeks and she appears withdrawn. Lost. I'm an asshole, generally speaking, but seeing her like this fucking hurts. I press play again and watch her shaky hands around the gun. So frightened. And then she cries out that if they don't kill her, she will shoot him. She wanted them to kill her. And that's the worst part of it. Did I drive her to this? Or was it something from her past?

I pull up the current video to check on her. Physically, she appears to be fine. Emotionally is an entirely different case. She sits huddled against the wall, as her eyes dart back and forth constantly, like she's looking for a threat to appear.

Finally, he pulls up to my property and parks at the back. Wasting no time, I race inside and down the stairs to the basement, finding my wife in the same spot, even though she has plenty of length on her chains. I'm not prepared for the emotions that all but attack me, when I gaze at her while we're both in the same room. The effect is more powerful than looking at my damn phone screen. I move to her and unlock the wrist restraints, and then the ones on her ankles. Her lashes flutter as she raises her gaze to mine. "Luca," she whispers, and I still can't figure out why I like hearing that so much from her, but I do. I'll never get enough of it.

I take her face in my hands as I kneel in front of her. "Butterfly. Beautiful Butterfly."

Slamming my lips to hers, I kiss her aggressively while she cries into my mouth, causing me to groan into hers. Athena lifts her hands and runs her fingers through my hair, and Jesus Christ, my wife makes me weak as hell, which is not something I can afford.

I ease one hand under her ass and the other around her back, and lift, as I rise and go up the stairs. She gazes at me in question. "Where are we going?"

Athena likely thinks I'm going to fuck her, and I want to more than I want to take my next breath, but right now there are more important things to deal with.

"For you to eat. You've been so bad, Butterfly. When I am not here, you are expected to take care of your basic needs. Every meal you were given, you refused."

"How?" She gasps. "They told you?"

I shake my head as I reach the kitchen. "Have you not learned yet? Cameras. They are everywhere."

Setting her on a chair at the table, I get her a plate of food, placing it in front of her, and I narrow my gaze at her. "Eat."

"I can't," she whispers so softly it's barely audible.

"Butterfly, I swear to you if you don't eat, you will regret it."

She sticks her fork into the steak, takes a bite and sets her fork down. "There, I ate," she says after she swallows her food.

"Athena," I warn.

I have no fucking clue why she isn't eating, but it won't be tolerated.

"I need to know, Luca. Did I kill him?"

Shaking my head, I say, "No. It's only a flesh wound. Eduardo will be just fine."

Placing her hand over her heart, she breathes a sigh of relief. "Thank God. I never meant to fire the gun."

Taking a seat across from her, I watch her continue to eat. "We'll be doing things differently. It's clear you cannot be left alone."

She glances at me and trembles slightly. "I'm sorry. It won't happen again."

I scowl at her. "No it won't, because I won't allow it. You could have hurt yourself, Butterfly."

"If you aren't leaving me alone, then what's going to happen to me?"

Smirking at her, I say, "You'll come with me wherever I go. It means you may see things you don't want to, but there's no other option."

Setting her fork down, she gazes at me. "I'm full."

I nod. "Come here."

Standing up, she walks over to me and I move my chair back, and pull her onto my lap. Placing my hand on her chin, I tilt her head back, forcing her eyes to meet mine. "Are you having flashbacks, Butterfly?"

"No," she whispers, and it's obvious to me she's lying. Whatever this Manny asshole did to her must have been worse than I knew. Eventually she'll open up to me and tell me everything, but for now I'll let it go.

"I'm mad at you," she breathes.

"I know, Butterfly."

Wrapping my arms around her waist, I pull her into my chest. She's reluctant at first, but eventually lays her head on my shoulder. With a long drawn out sigh, Athena says, "How can you miss someone you hate?"

I chuckle softly. "You can't. Wife, you don't hate me. You only wish you did."

"Something is obviously wrong with me," she says, and I feel the warmth of her breath on my neck, causing me to grit my teeth. I'm trying to not act like an animal, as she calls it, with her tonight but she's making my cock so hard, sitting on my lap like this.

"Why?"

She giggles softly. "You forced me to marry you. Kept me in a cage, then chained me to the wall, like someone does a pitbull they've grown tired of. Had sex with me whether I wanted it or not. I am nothing more than your captive. You don't care about me, but then I miss you when you're gone. I don't know what mental illness that is, but it's definitely one."

I grab her face in both my hands, and my voice comes out in a far more threatening growl than I intend. "You think I don't care about you? I was fucking terrified you were going to get hurt." I swallow hard. "Or worse. You are nothing more than my captive? You're my goddamn wife, and I'd lay down my life to protect you, without a second thought."

A tear rolls down her cheek, and I pull her closer, running my tongue up her cheek to taste her beautiful tear.

"Why do you do that?"

I groan quietly. "Because I'm obsessed with you, Butterfly. I want to take everything you have, including your tears. When I'm deep inside you, I want more. If I could crawl into your soul, I would. If you cry, I'll consume your tears. If you bleed, I'll take that too. There is no part of you I won't devour. Everything you have to give, I now own. I don't deserve it, but I'll take it anyway. Every man who has ever harmed you, dies. Anyone that considers it now, dies. Protecting you is the only thing that matters to me now."

I run my hand down her body until it settles on her stomach. "And our baby, that I have every intention of putting inside you."

Chapter Nineteen

ATHENA

Turning around on his lap, I straddle him while he watches me curiously. Leaning forward, I run my tongue up the side of his neck, thoroughly enjoying the groan it elicits.

"Bones," I moan, and he immediately corrects me.

"That's not my name for you, baby. The rest of the world knows me as Bones, but my wife calls me Luca. Always."

Dragging my fingers through his hair, I press my lips to his skin as his scent surrounds me. It's everything Luca. His heat. His smell. His hands digging into my hips.

My husband is everything I shouldn't desire, but do.

I scrape my teeth down his neck, and he growls as he grabs my hair. "Wife, you better stop if you don't want to be fucked."

Leaning forward, I whisper in his ear, "Luca, show me you missed me too."

He shivers beneath me, causing me to smile. My brain tells me to not become addicted to a monster, but my body says otherwise. Rising from the chair, he lifts me with him and sits me on the table, before taking my plate and putting it in the kitchen. He comes back with a glass, and sets it on the massive rectangular oak table. Grabbing the hem of my shirt, he lifts it over my head and tosses it on the far end of the table. He strokes his thumb over one of my nipples while he strokes his fingers down my cheek. "You're going to tell me to stop, and that it's too much, but I won't. I want to hear you scream. Lay down."

After I lie back, he hooks his thumbs into my shorts and pulls them down my legs. "Tomorrow we are going shopping, because my wife deserves her own clothing. Tonight, you won't need any."

He stares at me with heat in his eyes as he removes his shirt, revealing his upper body that makes my thighs clench with need.

"Luca."

After removing his pants, he grips his large cock, and I lick my lips as he chuckles softly. "Not yet, Butterfly. You had your dinner, and now it's my turn."

Leaning over me, he presses his lips to mine and kisses me slowly at first, but then it turns desperate, as he licks at my tongue. I run my hands through his hair and he groans. Pulling back, he pops an ice cube from the glass into his mouth, and smirks at me like he knows something I don't.

Luca runs his tongue, and the ice cube, all over my neck and down to my nipple. I arch my back as he alternates between the ice and his tongue. He moves to the other side and repeats the torture. When he moves to my abdomen, I shiver from the cold ice cube, run my hands into his hair and pull at the strands. "Please, Luca."

He drags his tongue up the inside of my thigh, and down the other, as I tremble from anticipation.

"So needy and so fucking beautiful."

Swiping his tongue along my slit, my back arches from the cold contact, because even though the ice has melted, it's still cool. He flicks his tongue over my clit with a quick motion. The cool turns to warm, as I cry out for him.

Suddenly he stops, while staring at me with a heated gaze. "Beg for more, Butterfly."

"What?" I pant shamelessly.

"Beg."

"Please, Luca," I say, as I attempt to push his head back down.

He chuckles softly, and his breath on my clit only makes it throb more. "Such a needy girl."

Watching me intently, he pushes two fingers inside me and I moan loudly.

"Good girl, let me hear you."

Taking my clit between his lips, he sucks hard, while he pulls his fingers out and slams them back inside me with blinding force. "Luca," I cry out loudly.

Reaching up, he pinches my nipple with his free hand, and the relief I've been craving hits me. I buck my hips up while my back arches off the table. He removes his fingers from my pussy, and inserts his tongue deep inside me, swirling it around while he pinches my clit and, he was right, it's too much.

"Stop."

He chuckles softly. "Not a chance, Butterfly. Come again."

I don't know what's wrong with me, but the intensity is more than I can handle, and tears spring to my eyes, which only causes Luca to go feral.

"Fuck," he grunts, as he rises to his feet and slams his cock inside me. Leaning over me, he licks at my tears. "I know I shouldn't, but I fucking love it when you cry for me."

Suddenly I break out into a fit of giggles. "That's probably a red flag."

He smirks at me. "You're not wrong."

Leaning down, he takes my nipple into his mouth and swipes his tongue across it, like he did my clit, and I shudder in response. I place my hands on his shoulders while he rocks back and forth and shakes his head. "I had every intention of eating that pussy all night long. Then I remembered how good you feel."

"Luca."

He takes both my wrists and presses them against the table over my head, and I quickly spiral. Screaming, "No," I cry as I tremble. He lets go of my hands and grabs my face, forcing me to look into his eyes. "I don't know what the fuck that asshole did to you, but you're safe with me."

I want to tell him it wasn't Manny. My life in hell began long before I met him. I will never tell him, because as much as I wanted to hate him, I don't. And I know if I tell him, he'll be disgusted with me, like I am with myself. Luca will never look at me again the way he does now. I learned that difficult lesson a long time ago.

I glance at my first boyfriend, William. He loves me, so I know he'll help. After I tell him what my father has been doing to me, his response is unexpected. He retracts his hand from mine. "That's fucking disgusting."

"It's not what I want," I whisper as I hang my head down.

"Your own father?"

His words are harsh, but it's the way he looks at me that embeds itself in my soul.

"Looking at you makes me want to vomit."

He pushes me to my knees. "Since you enjoy being a whore, I'll treat you like one."

"Butterfly, stay with me. You are fucking safe."

Gripping my chin with his hand makes me focus on him. "I'm not a good man. It's the complete opposite. I swear to you, no man will ever hurt you again. You are married to a man born into vengeance. I can't promise to always do the right thing, but I can, and do, promise to always protect you from assholes like Manny."

"Luca, make me forget he exists."

Again, I'm not talking about Manny, but he doesn't need to know that.

He presses his lips to mine and thrusts his tongue in my mouth, as he begins to move inside me again.

Tilting my head to the side, he deepens our kiss, and I run my fingers through his hair. I don't understand my own emotions. The man who has held me captive, and kept me in a cage, is a place of safety to me. I should be terrified of him, but I'm not.

He pulls back and stares at me, while he picks up his speed. "Mine," he growls, and I nod in agreement, because I want to be his. I want him to always look at me like he'll die if he can't have me.

His abs tighten as he buries his face in my neck, and grunts against my skin. He fills me, and I feel his cock spasming inside me.

Lifting his head, he stares at me with a serious expression. "No more not eating. When I put my baby inside you, I want it born healthy. You'll take care of yourself, Butterfly."

"What if I don't want a baby?"

He pulls out of me with a chuckle. "You'll get used to the idea. You're my wife, and you will have my children."

It's not that I don't want children, I do, but I don't want to do to my children what was done to me. What if I'm like my mother, and abandon my child because it's easier? Sure, my father is an abusive asshole, but she could've taken me when she ran, but going without her child was the easy route. Would I decide I don't want to be married to the head of a mafia family, and leave my child behind? I want to believe I could never do such a thing, but maybe it's in my DNA. My grandmother abandoned my mother, and my mother abandoned me. Why wouldn't I expect I'd do the same?

"If you love your future children, you don't want me to be their mother."

He helps me off the table and I shrug. "I don't see myself as the mothering type."

Pulling me into his arms, he smirks. "You will have all the help you need. You want a nanny? Done. Two Nannies? Done. A chef? Already have one. A housekeeper? Also have one of those."

Carrying me up the stairs, he says, "Mothering my children is part of your job as my wife. I'll do whatever I can to make it easier on you, but there's no way it isn't happening. Generally speaking, the first born male takes over the family. So if one of my idiot brothers has one first, everything is fucked. This is important; if it weren't, I wouldn't require it of you."

Required.

I don't bother arguing, because if I've learned anything about Luca, it's that what he says will be done, will be. If I'm ever allowed to leave alone, I'll get on birth control until I decide I want a child. Maybe I never will. I honestly don't believe he'll hurt me if I can never bear children.

He fills up the bathtub with bubbles, water, and tells me to get in with a nod of his head. I do and he climbs in behind me, and wraps his arms around me.

I lay back against his chest and sigh, as the warm water and scent of lavender soothes me.

"Are you going to tell me what he did to you?"

"No."

He chuckles. "You will eventually, wife. I'll be everything in your world. One day, you'll trust me and expose your soul to me."

I want to tell him I won't, but it's not because I don't trust him, but because I know he'll be so disgusted with me, he'll never touch me again. The thought of him looking at me the way William did, or taunting like Manny used to, is something I know I can't handle.

Chapter Twenty
BONES

I'm determined to find out what the hell she went through, so I know how to be there for her. I know she's experiencing flashbacks. Is she having nightmares? How frequently does Manny cross her mind? It pisses me off, because I don't want any man inside her head. Making her fucking cry. Those tears belong to me and me alone. She turns in the bathtub so her chest is pressed against mine, and I stroke my fingers down her back. I can't help myself, there is never a time when I don't need to be touching her.

"Are there any stores you like?"

"What?" she squeaks adorably.

I wrap my arms around her, holding her tight. "We are going shopping tomorrow. Are there stores you like to shop at?"

She giggles against my skin. "Luca, I haven't been shopping since I don't even remember when. Target or Walmart are fine."

Wrapping her hair around my fist, I pull her head back, and force her to look at me. "My wife is not shopping at Walmart. You will have the best of everything."

She flashes me a smile that makes my chest squeeze, and I don't know why. "Like in *Pretty Woman*? I'm no *Julia Roberts*, but that looked like so much fun."

I groan as I release her hair. "Silly wife, she has nothing on you. There's no woman more beautiful than you."

Athena grins as she blushes. "Careful, Luca. I might start thinking you like me."

As much as I planned to feel nothing for her, she made it impossible. Does she actually believe I don't even like her? I have trouble imagining anyone could meet Athena, and not genuinely like her.

I clear my throat. "Are you ready to get out?"

Her face falls, and as much as I enjoy her tears, this expression I don't like. If I'm honest with myself, and I don't want to be, I prefer her smiles and laughter. This is exactly what De Luca warned me about. We both stand and get out of the tub. I wrap her in a warm white towel, and she races out of the bathroom like it's on fire.

I dry myself off and head into the bedroom, climbing into the bed beside her. She turns away from me. "I'm tired. I'm going to sleep."

I wrap my arm around her and pull her into me. "You think I don't like you, Butterfly? When I got the call in Vegas that you got a hold of a gun, if you were any other woman, I would've instructed them to shoot you. I would not have hesitated, and I sure as hell would not have been panicking the way I was."

She turns over in my arms, puts her arm around me, and kisses my chest. I clench my jaw and groan through my teeth. "You better go to sleep."

With a giggle, Athena says, "Are you thinking about sex again?"

I admit to her, "There are very few moments of the day when I'm not thinking about being inside your beautiful pussy."

Tilting her head back, she glances at me with a slight smile, and the moonlight outside shines just enough to see a beautiful blush appear on her cheeks. "I don't hate that."

Placing my hand on the side of her neck, I pull her closer and kiss her softly.

"Go to sleep, beautiful wife."

I move to my back and take her with me, holding her close, and she rests her head on my chest with a sweet little moan.

When I witnessed Manny assaulting her on video, I knew I'd protect her. There is no reasoning behind how much it infuriated me, watching him with his hands on Athena. I had already decided she'd be my wife, so maybe that's why I was driven to inflict so much pain on him. The truth is, Manny was going to die regardless, because he sent her to steal from me. Had I not needed to get married, I would've killed her too without an ounce of remorse. Yet now, as I look at my sleeping wife, it's more than that. No woman has ever made me feel a goddamn thing beyond an orgasm. She does. She makes me feel things I am not fucking comfortable with. I close my eyes, trying to push all this bullshit out of my mind, and eventually fall into a deep sleep with my wife in my arms.

Waking up, I reach around for my wife, but she's not here. Immediately, I consider she has once again attempted to run. Rising out of the bed, I grab a pair of sweatpants and pull them on, before making my way downstairs to look for Athena.

I stand in the entryway to the kitchen, staring at my wife. Fuck, she's gorgeous. She is wearing tiny black shorts and a white tank top; my sister's clothing from when she stayed here last summer, but we're going to correct Athena not having her own clothes today. Her dark hair is pulled into a high ponytail. She moves around the kitchen, swaying her sexy ass with every movement, as she makes pancakes and bacon. I fold my arms over my chest as I watch her like a hawk. She stares at the pancakes and grumbles, "What kind of idiot can't make pancakes?"

"Good morning, wife."

She jumps with a start. "Oh my God. You scared me, Luca. I'm making you breakfast. Do you like pancakes and bacon?"

I smirk at her with a nod, which is a complete lie. I don't remember the last time I even ate this early. However, if my wife makes me breakfast, I'll eat it.

"Your coffee is on the table. I'll bring your food in just a moment."

"Do you need help, Butterfly?"

Her cheeks turn bright red as she giggles. "There's no help for me at this point. The pancakes are a little overcooked, and the bacon is," she waves her hand in the air, "crispy."

I attempt to give her a reassuring smile. "I'm sure it'll be delicious."

Walking over to the table, I take a seat and sip my coffee. She brings out a plate of food and sets it in front of me. I glance at the food and then at her. "Thank you, wife."

I shake my head when she goes back to the kitchen and can't see me, because this food is not overcooked. It's burnt. I'm not sure how you even achieve the blackness of these pancakes. Athena comes in with her own plate and sets it down, before she takes a seat across from me. She glances at her food. "Don't eat that. This is terrible."

I cut a piece of the charred pancake and pop it into my mouth as she gapes at me. I chew and swallow. "It's delicious. Thank you."

Athena giggles as she holds a piece of bacon in her hand, staring at it like it personally offended her. "There is no way you think this is delicious."

I keep eating with an exaggerated, "Mmmm."

Had anybody else made this food I'd refuse to eat it, but when my wife goes out of her way to make a meal for me, I'll eat it. Whether it's pleasing to the palate or not.

We continue eating in silence, and if she notices me staring at her she doesn't say anything. My eyes are always on her. She's stunning and no matter what I do, I can't get enough of her.

"You seem happier today."

Her smile makes her face glow as she responds, "I'm excited to go outside today."

I grab my plate and she grabs hers and follows me into the kitchen.

"You can always go outside whenever you want to, Butterfly. If I'm not here, take Jimmy with you. As long as someone is with you, it's fine."

She shakes her head. "I'd rather stay inside. He doesn't like me very much."

I chuckle, because she's probably right since she shot Eduardo, but it doesn't matter.

"It's his job to protect you, and I promise he will do what he's instructed to."

We put our plates in the dishwasher, and I pull her into my arms and hold her close. She wraps her hands around my waist with a tiny sigh. "I'm sorry about breakfast, Luca."

I kiss her on the top of her head. "Don't be. I'm not. It was perfect, like you. Let me get ready and we'll go shopping."

She squeals with delight, making my chest squeeze tight. I don't know how it happened, but seeing my wife happy has turned into everything, seemingly overnight. I kiss her neck and break away from her, and go upstairs to get ready for our day out. I had no idea she had wanted to go outside so badly, but I should have. Nobody wants to be kept locked up in a house the way she has been. As I walk up the stairs, I decide to not only take her shopping, but make an entire day of it. While I have work I need to do, seeing my beautiful wife happy right now is priority number one.

Chapter Twenty-One
ATHENA

Luca watches me as I move through the store, like at any moment he's expecting a bullet to come barreling through the air toward me, and he'll be the one to stop it before it kills me. It might be a little much, but also, it's nice to think he cares at all. He holds up a gorgeous black dress. "Do you like this?"

I take the price tag in my hand, and my eyes widen in sticker shock. "Three thousand dollars for a dress, Luca?"

He smirks at me. "I didn't ask if you approved of the cost, Butterfly. I asked if you liked it."

Shaking my head with disapproval, I say, "Obviously. It's beautiful, but too much."

He hands it to the cashier. "Add this to the others."

Coming up behind me, he wraps his arms around me and kisses my neck softly.

"Money is not an object for you, Butterfly. I will tell you if it's too much, but I guarantee you, it never will be."

He turns me in his arms so I'm facing him, and lifts my chin with his thumb and forefinger.

"I want you to understand. I am a billionaire several times over. Everything I have is yours, so you are a billionaire as well. We will have problems like anybody else, but money will not be an issue. Butterfly, you are stunning, and you should have beautiful clothes."

This probably shouldn't be an issue, but I worry about the future. When I was really little, my parents would argue about my mother shopping too much. And I don't want to end up like they did. He doesn't know that, and I can't tell him, because I don't want to have a conversation about my parents with him.

"Understood?" He asks and I roll my eyes at him. Immediately, he arches an eyebrow as he hands me a purple dress. "Go try this on. Now."

His voice comes out stern, and almost threatening, so I go to the change room. When I move to close the door behind me, he stops it from closing and smirks at me. "Put your hands on the wall, Butterfly."

"Luca," I breathe and he glares at me. "Now, Athena. Don't make me tell you again."

I walk to the other side of the large dressing room and place my hands on the light blue wall, as he comes up behind me and runs his hand down my back to my ass. Leaning his head over my shoulder, he whispers in my ear, "My wife would never roll her eyes at me, would she?"

"I'm sorry."

He chuckles. "Are you?"

Hooking his thumbs into my shorts, he pulls them down to the floor and I complain, "Luca, there are people in the store."

There aren't many. A few of his security guys, and two people working in the store, but still, we aren't alone.

Running two fingers along my slit, he groans, "They won't complain. Do you know how much money they're making from this sale? You were rude to me, wife. Now you get the opportunity to make it up to me."

"How?"

He growls in my ear, "By coming all over my cock."

The sound of his belt is loud in the change room as he undoes his pants. I place my hands on the mirror, and he says, "Good girl," proving that is what he wanted.

I look in the mirror as he nudges my thighs further apart with his leg. He pushes into me with one hard thrust, causing me to gasp from the intrusion.

He wraps his hand around my throat as he fucks me from behind. This is not new for him, he's done this many times, but it's the first time I can see it with my own eyes. I stare at the skull tattoo on his hand, and realize how beautiful it is. A black skull with a dark purple rose in one of the eye sockets. Mesmerizing.

"Butterfly," he groans, as he pulls out most of the way and slams back inside me.

I bite my lip as an orgasm threatens to make me scream, and immediately he scolds me, "I don't think so, wife. I want to hear you."

Releasing my lip, I cry out, hoping nobody else hears me as I tremble against the mirror. "Good girl."

He picks up his speed, and when I spot his clenched jaw in the mirror, I know he's close. As much as I enjoy how he makes me feel physically, this is my favorite part. The pleasure in his gaze, the slight parting of his lips, and the sexy grunt that escapes. That and when he spasms inside me.

"Fuck, wife. Every goddamn time you feel better than the time before."

Pulling out of me, he spins me around and grabs my face, aggressively pressing his lips to mine. His kiss is desperate, like he didn't just fuck me.

He pulls my shorts up before putting himself back into his pants. Ignoring his smug grin, I ask, "Do you want me to try on the dress?"

Luca shrugs his shoulders. "If you need to. I don't care, I just wanted to fuck my beautiful wife."

"You're an animal."

He chuckles softly. "I know I am, baby. Are we pretending you don't like it?"

"No."

The truth is, even the first time, when I told him no and fought him, I wanted him even then. My husband is hot as hell, and I can't imagine any woman turning him down. Of course I did because I was trying to get away from him, and that goddamn cage.

Luca steps closer to me and leans his head down. "That's unfortunate. I thought I was going to need to remind you how much you love it."

He stares at me with a heated expression, the kind that makes me forget to breathe.

"If you forget, I'm happy to remind you, Butterfly."

When I don't respond, because I can barely even breathe, he grins. "Come on. Let's go get lunch."

Luca grabs the dress off the hook he put it on, and I follow him out of the dressing room and glance at the four other people in the store, and wonder if they heard us. I blush as we stand at the counter and he hands the lady his Amex Black Card. The blonde woman glances at him and bats her eyelashes, and when she gives him the total and it's almost thirty thousand dollars, I almost vomit. I grab his arm. "Luca, no."

He glares at me. "Not now, Athena."

His security guys grab the bags, as we walk out of the store and head back to the waiting car. Luca opens the back of the Range Rover and I slide in. He pulls out his wallet and gets in beside me. Taking out another credit card, he hands it to me. "This is yours. If you want to shop online, or one day when you're shopping by yourself, use it. You never need to worry about reaching a limit. I don't want to ever hear a complaint about how much money I spend on my wife. If I didn't want to do it, or couldn't afford it, I wouldn't spend it. The fact is, I have more money than I can possibly spend in my lifetime, or in our children's lifetime."

I take the card, and put it in my purse without further conversation about it, because this seems to be something that pisses him off. At some point, I'm sure I'll fight with him about things. When they matter. I'll choose my battles, but I'm sure bigger things than money will come up. I realize a lot of women would kill to trade places with me financially. Most people struggle with money, and they don't have a husband spending a down payment on a house on clothing. It's ridiculous to get upset about.

"Thank you."

He closes his eyes, like those two words are pleasurable.

"You're my wife, and I want to take care of you without argument. I know you haven't always had a man to do that, and I want to be that for you."

I snort laugh. "I've never had that, Luca."

"How did you end up with Manny?" He asks as the driver pulls away from the curb.

I avert my eyes, not really wanting to have this conversation, because there's something about him that makes me feel safe and I know better. You can say too much, and I need to be careful not to.

"Talk to me, Butterfly."

I take in a deep breath and release it. "Boy meets girl. He promises her the world, and then destroys her. It started with verbal attacks, but over time it became physical. At first it was once every couple of months, but it wasn't long before it became daily. He wanted me to start stealing things so he could sell them. I agreed at first, because I felt like I had to. Manny bought me food a few days a week, and paid for the hotel in exchange for the items."

Luca stares at me with obvious irritation. "How much of a cut did you take?"

I shake my head. "None."

He closes his eyes tight and clenches his fists.

"I wish he were still alive, so I could fucking kill him."

With a long drawn out sigh, I say, "Well, you already did that. You broke his bones. Who does that?"

His eyes pop open and he grins. "Me. I do that, and I'd gladly do it again if I could."

"How did you start that?"

113

Taking my hand in his, he smiles softly. "It happened by accident. It's hard to explain it without scaring the hell out of you."

I move over and climb onto his lap. "Tell me. Please."

Luca wraps his arms around me, pulling my body close to his. "It happened by accident. I was in a fight as a teenager with the son of a rival family. The sound of his arm breaking, I liked it, and knew I'd hurt someone again by doing the same thing. I learned how to break bones with ease. There are a million ways to physically hurt someone. Guns, knives, but breaking someone's bones means more pain, because you can administer an awful lot of anguish before they die. A gun or a knife will kill much quicker. And I'm rarely looking to kill someone with speed."

He notices the expression on my face and says, "I'll never do that to you. Ever. I'll never cause you physical pain you don't want."

I chew on my bottom lip nervously. "And the cage?"

Luca runs his fingers down my cheek, with a tenderness I didn't know he was capable of. "Butterfly, never again. I swear to you, never. I will die before I ever do that to you again. The same goes for the chains."

I kiss him softly. "Thank you, Luca. Thank you."

He shakes his head when I pull away. "That's not something you should be thanking me for. One day you'll tell me why the cage is that terrible for you. Nobody likes being trapped in a cage, but your reaction tells me you had experience with it."

I nod in agreement instead of denying it. "Far too much experience, Luca, and one day I will, but I'm not ready."

It's pure torture to finally have someone that makes it feel like you can lay all your baggage at their feet. There's nothing I want more than to trust him with everything. My past is not for the faint of heart. And the only thing worse than the memories that haunt me, would be if I lost him now when he has made me realize I want him. Not just his body, all of him. And I wish I could give myself to him completely. It's just too risky.

Chapter Twenty-Two
Bones

I grab the purple dress and heels I bought for Athena, and instruct her to put them on.

She gapes at me in shock. "Luca, people will see."

I chuckle lightly. "No, wife. They won't. The windows are tinted dark enough, it's impossible to see inside. Now get changed, so I can take you on a proper date."

The sweet smile on her face tells me I chose the right word. Her fighting stops immediately, and she does as she's told. Of course, I catch glimpses of her naked body as she puts the dress on. She will rarely have complete privacy when I'm around, because I can't help myself. My wife is a feast for the eyes, and I won't restrain myself with her.

"Pervert," she says, when she catches me watching her.

I take her face in my hands and kiss her quickly. "You're mine, Butterfly. And I'll look at you any time I damn well please, which turns out to be a lot."

She rolls her eyes at me and I arch my eyebrow, but am not truly mad. Athena covers her mouth with her hand, when she realizes her indiscretion. "I'm sorry."

"Come on, brat."

I step out of the vehicle first, and after she scoots closer, I lift her out of the car as she giggles. I'm sure she is capable of getting out on her own, but I'll take every opportunity to have my hands on her. Placing my arm around her waist, we head over to the upscale restaurant, and walk to the wrought iron patio. It's less fancy than inside, but I thought she'd like to eat outside and enjoy the sun, rather than being stuck in a building. It's clear I made the right decision when she turns to me with a beaming smile. "Thank you, Luca."

We take a seat at a large black wrought iron table, with a large matching umbrella over it. There is no one else out here other than us, and there won't be. I bought out the entire restaurant so we'd be alone. If she notices the lack of patrons, she doesn't say anything about it. The waitress brings over two glasses of wine and two menus. I could have ordered for both of us ahead of time, and I considered it, but I want to know what she'll order for herself. I have a strong desire to know everything about my wife.

The waitress walks away, and Athena picks up her glass and takes a tentative sip of wine. She sets her glass down and licks her lips. "That's good. Fruity. Sweet, but not too sweet."

"Do you not normally drink wine?"

She shakes her head. "No."

I'm tempted to push for more information, but I don't.

"What are you going to order?"

Athena shifts in her seat uncomfortably. "I don't know. What are you getting?"

She stares down at the menu as I answer her, "Steak and a baked potato."

Closing the menu, she smiles at me, but it doesn't reach her eyes. "That sounds good. I'll get the same thing."

Her entire demeanor has changed in a heartbeat for no apparent reason. She now sits slumped, with her head hanging down, like she's ashamed of something and it concerns me.

"Butterfly, look at me."

Athena lifts her head, meeting my gaze, as I take her hand in mine. "Is everything okay?"

She swallows hard and nods. "Yeah, I'm good. Thank you for this. It's nice here."

Lifting her hand, I bring it to my lips and kiss her skin softly. "You know you can talk to me about anything, right?"

Taking a sip of her wine, she sets it back down and looks around her. "I'm okay, Luca."

The waitress comes and takes our orders, as well as our menus, and heads back inside.

"My mom wants us to come over for dinner in a few weeks."

Her head pops up. "I'd like that. She seemed sweet. Can I ask a question about something?"

I nod while I stroke her hand. "You can ask me anything, Butterfly. If it's not dangerous for me to answer, I will."

"Are you mad at Penelope?"

Chuckling loudly, I say, "No. I'm also not surprised. If I thought there was any chance she'd overhear my conversation with my father, she would not have been there. Penelope has never accepted where our father gets the ridiculous amount of money he gives to her. She thinks we are terrible men, and I have no doubt her heart was in the right place."

She stares at me nervously. "So you're not going to hurt her?"

I shake my head as I laugh again. "No. My mother would kill me. And there's nothing more important than family. Had she not been my sister, the answer might be different."

The waitress brings our food and we both start eating. In between bites, she asks, "If they call you Bones because that's what you do, what about your brothers?"

"Do they break bones too?" She adds.

I chuckle. "No, Butterfly. Well, they have, but it's not what they're known for. Kage, well, let's just say, had he found you breaking into his home, you'd still be inside that metal prison you hate so much."

She swallows a bite of steak. "And the others?"

I'm honestly not sure she wants to know about the other two, but she asked. Rule number one with me is, don't ask a question if you can't handle the answer, because I will be honest.

117

"Psycho is known as Psycho because it describes him well. He tends to not consider consequences for his actions, and doesn't think things through. Psycho could easily start a mafia war because of it, and get us all killed. He'll go in guns blazing, without first getting information as to who, and how many, are in the room. He's dangerous."

"And Reaper?" She asks with a raised brow, and I swallow my food before responding. "Reaper is a serial killer. He doesn't work with us, which is unfortunate, because he is both lethal and brutal."

She sets her fork down and stares at me with complete shock. "A serial killer? Like he kills people who have done things to him?"

I chuckle lightly. "Sure. But not just that. There's a certain thrill when taking someone's life. You won't understand. It's powerful. Most of us restrain ourselves, and only kill when necessary. Reaper is not like the rest of us."

Athena swallows hard as she tries to process this information. "Just women?"

I shake my head. "He's an equal opportunist. Men. Women. The only difference is he doesn't fuck the men before killing them."

Taking another bite of steak, she chews and swallows slowly. "Interesting family, Luca."

Shrugging my shoulders, I say. "Very. Now tell me about yours."

Her eyes meet mine before quickly glancing away. "My father's name is Alex, and he works with money. I don't honestly know what he does beyond that."

"Your mother?"

That's really what I want to know about, because aren't daughters normally close to their mothers? Why is my wife not on the news, with her mother frantically searching for her? Begging for her safe return. That would be a normal response, since she came to my property to rob me and never left. Until today.

"I don't know her. She left when I was five."

Athena swipes a tear from her cheek, as I ask, "Where did she go?"

She looks at me with such anguish in her eyes. "I don't know, Luca. She just left. Her and my father were fighting about something. And the next morning she was gone. Then everything changed."

I sit silently, waiting to see if she'll give me more than that, but she doesn't. Instead, my wife sits here eating and drinking in complete silence. She's done sharing, I can see it on her face. It's like she shuts it down, as she forces a smile on her face.

"Thank you for lunch, Luca. This has been wonderful."

I scoot my chair back. "Come here."

Without any hesitation, she gets up and walks over to me. I pull her onto my lap and run my hand through her hair, and she closes her eyes like it's the most pleasure she's ever experienced.

Pressing my lips to hers, she whimpers as I slide my tongue into her mouth, caressing hers slowly. With my hand in her hair, I tilt her head to the side and deepen our kiss. People walk down the busy street, but I pay them no attention. My wife is the only thing that matters to me at this moment. She's quickly becoming the entire center of my world. If anybody tries to take what's mine, I know I won't simply break their bones. They would experience the most horrific pain they can even imagine. I'd burn the entire world to the ground to keep her safe. Domenic was right. Athena has destroyed everything I thought I knew about myself. I never wanted this, a wife, but now that I have her, there's nothing I wouldn't do to hold onto her.

I pull back from our kiss, and she's so beautiful. Athena looks slightly dazed, her lips plump from being kissed, her eyes wide with lust, and a slight blush on her cheeks. She runs her fingers down my face and sighs softly. Not from annoyance, but I think from contentment. "Luca," she whispers softly. I could listen to her say my name like that all fucking day long. I've always preferred Bones over my actual given name. Nobody, aside from my parents, has called me Luca in over twenty-five years. Hearing my wife say it does things to me I never saw coming. Athena, for me, is like someone has been holding my head under water for the longest time. She's like finally being able to breathe again when I thought I never would.

"There's a bookstore up the street. I thought maybe you'd like to get a few to keep you busy when I'm working."

For the life of me, I don't understand why her face turns white as a ghost.

"I don't really like to read. I prefer TV."

I nod my understanding, but to be honest, I can't imagine choosing to not read. It's one of my favorite things to do when I have time, which unfortunately isn't often. I assumed it's something everyone loves, but clearly I was wrong.

"Is there anything else you'd like to do before we go home?"

She shakes her head no, and I kiss her on the neck.

"I've ordered a laptop for you."

Again, the look on her face confuses me, but as always she's secretive and unwilling to say a damn thing. It's frustrating. Under normal circumstances, I'd put her in the damn cage until she starts talking, but I can't do that. Threatening her will not get her to talk. The only thing that will accomplish is driving her away from me. It makes me feel powerless, and that's not something I'm accustomed to.

Chapter Twenty-Three
ATHENA

I'm freaking out on the inside, while trying to appear calm and collected. He is asking too many questions, and I'm terrified he's going to begin to piece things together. Luca has become the man of any woman's dreams. I never would've imagined the man that held me captive, and planned to kill me, would be capable of this. He is good to me. Any other woman would be thrilled to get a brand new laptop. I'm afraid that stupid electronic is going to be the beginning of everything unraveling. I have no doubt Luca is going to question why I'm not using it. I can't tell him the truth, because he'll ask why. I can almost hear him now.

"Why can't you read, Butterfly?"

When he mentioned getting me books, I panicked. I told him I don't like to read, because telling him the truth was mortifying. Everybody can read. Everybody but me. It's interesting that I was willing to do anything to get away from him, but now the thought of losing Luca is debilitating.

"I have some work to do. I'll only be a few hours," he says as we pull up to the house.

I smile. "That's fine. I'm sure you have bones to break. Your fingers must be getting twitchy."

He chuckles loudly. "My fingers have found other things more useful. I'll be in my office, not breaking bones."

We walk into the house, and he turns to me and strokes his fingers down my face. "I'll be down soon, Butterfly. Make yourself at home. My home is yours."

He kisses me quickly before he walks away and goes upstairs.

I kick off my shoes and settle onto the couch, and stare at the mural on the ceiling. My mother used to tell me stories about Greek mythology. It's how I got my name. She was fascinated with it, but now as I stare at the pictures, it causes bile to rise in my throat. How could she leave her child in that hell?

Footsteps approach and Jimmy appears. "You have a guest, Mrs. Bonetti," he says with a sick smile on his face.

A guest? I literally don't know anyone, so that doesn't make any sense to me. Penelope, maybe? Perhaps she wants to make sure I'm okay.

I nod as another set of footsteps echo in the distance, until they stop, and all the air in my lungs escapes. I tremble and cannot breathe. This isn't happening. It's a nightmare.

"Princess. I've missed you."

My head screams 'no, no, no,' but nothing comes out of my mouth. I'm unable to speak.

"Time to go home," he says.

I shake my head, and finally find the ability to speak. "I live here now."

He chuckles with a sinister grin. "This entire building is lined with explosives outside. If you come with me, Bonetti is safe, but if you refuse, you'll die together."

I glance at Jimmy, hoping he's going to save us, but he laughs. "Don't look to me to save you, bitch."

My father looks at me. "What's it going to be, Princess?"

I hang my head down. "I'll go. Don't hurt Luca. I'll do anything."

He nods. "Let's go."

I rise off the couch and go to put my shoes on, but he says, "Don't bother. You won't need those."

As I move closer, he grips the back of my neck hard, and we walk out of the only safe place I've ever known.

I love you, Luca.

I don't say it out loud, because it will only anger my father. My dad is a monster regardless of his mood, but when he's angry, it's

122

absolutely terrifying. We walk down the steps to a large white van and he opens the door. "Get in."

Glancing back at the house, I get into the van as my entire world crumbles. He will make sure I never get away again. Luca thinks all my trauma is because of what Manny did to me, but he was child's play compared to what my father does to me.

I watch as he hands Jimmy a stack of money, before he gets into the driver's seat and begins driving away. It's devastating to me that I know Luca will think I ran away from him after the perfect day.

My father gazes at me from the mirror. "You're going to die in my house, Princess. You aren't going to the basement this time. You'll be in the hot attic. If he comes looking for you, he'll look in the basement, but he'll never think to look up there. No one will ever see you again. You did this to yourself."

He thinks death is a punishment, but it's not. I welcome it. Pray for it. My only wish is for it to come quickly. I know him well, so there's no suspense as to what he has planned. I already know. This is my version of hell. And there's no way out. No one to save me. My little slice of happiness is over now.

I stare out the window on the two hour drive to my final resting place. The trees whir by as we drive further into the country. Before long there's nothing but grass and trees, as far as the eye can see. There are no other cars anymore. It's just us alone in a rural area nobody even knows about. We pull up to my house of horrors, and a tear trickles down my cheek. I know what comes next, and it causes bile to rise in my throat.

He puts the vehicle in park and gets out, and opens my door. "We're home. Are you excited?"

As always, he grips the back of my neck hard, until I cry out from the pain, and orders, "Walk."

I walk up the wood steps to the farmhouse, and he opens the door and I go through it, with him right behind me.

"You remember where the attic is, Princess?"

Without a word, I walk straight through the dimly lit hallway to the attic, which is above the hallway of bedrooms. He pulls on the dingy cord and the stairs appear. I walk up the creaky steps, and glance around the room I haven't seen since my mother was here. It's different now though. It used to have chests full of memories, but he's changed things. Now there sits a metal cage, probably big enough for a large dog, but not much more.

He comes up behind me. "Take your dress off."

"I came with you without a fight. Please don't do this."

My father grins at me. "You need to be punished."

I stare at his gray hair and bushy eyebrows, and his blue eyes that match mine bore into me. "Do as you're told, or it's going to be worse."

The tears fall as I remove my dress, and he groans in pleasure. It's not like when Luca does it, this time it's not a turn on, it's disgusting. Revolting. There's a lot I don't know about society, but even I know this is not okay. However, my father does not, or simply doesn't care.

"On your knees for daddy."

As much as it is the last thing I want to do, I kneel. I don't want to, but what I want doesn't matter.

He grips my chin in his hand, lifting my head, as he forces me to look at him. "I failed you, Princess. I should have punished you more, taught you what was acceptable, and what was not. I'll correct that now."

Walking over to the corner, he picks something up and walks back over to me. It's a large black leather made item. I think it's a whip. Soon enough he confirms it. "I'm going to whip you, and then you'll learn to do as you're told."

The first hit across my chest steals all the air from my lungs. He moves to my back and does the same there. The pain is unreal. I close my eyes and picture Luca's face looking at me. This is how I'll get through this, by leaving my body. The blinding pain punctures my perfect picture of my husband, and I scream his name, "Luca!"

My father laughs. "He can't save you. Do you think you're the only slut he was fucking? He'll be deep inside someone else before today even ends."

He drops the whip at his feet and unbuckles his pants as I sob, and he drops his pants to the floor, revealing the dick that literally makes my stomach turn.

"Open your mouth, Princess. Show daddy how sorry you are."

I do, and he does what he always does. He fucks my mouth. My own father violates me in the worst possible way. But I'm not the same girl I was, so when he finishes, I hold it in my mouth. He kneels and grabs my face. "Fucking swallow," he screams angrily. His face is less than an inch from mine as I spit his cum in his face.

"You fucking bitch," he says, right before he punches me in the face repeatedly. I fall over, and he grabs my hair and pulls me to the cage. "Get in."

My face hurts, as does my head. The pain is excruciating, and I know this will happen again and again. Whatever fight I had is gone. I crawl into the cage and he locks me in. Now I'm waiting, hoping that I'll die. I have no doubt my father will follow through on his threats to kill me, but it won't be anytime soon. He'll use me, and abuse me as much as he can, before I breathe my last breath.

Chapter Twenty-Four
BONES

Listening to my father for two hours was difficult. He even sounds weak. However, it was business as usual for him. He is exhausted, but he won't slow down until he's dead. I feel like a horrible son for thinking I hope it's sooner rather than later. I'll miss him terribly, but I hate knowing he's in so much pain. He'll be informing my mother and brothers later today. My poor mom is going to be devastated.

I head downstairs to find my wife, with the plan to lose myself in her. She somehow makes everything feel manageable. When I make it to the large living room I spot her shoes on the floor, but she's not in sight. I check the kitchen and she's not there either.

"Athena," I call out, but there's no response.

After going upstairs and checking the bedroom, I begin to worry. Where the fuck is she? I head to my office to look at the security cameras. My entire property is fitted with, not only cameras everywhere, but motion detectors. If she is in this house, I will find her.

I pull up the live feed on every single camera, one at a time, before I finally admit to myself that she's not here. She left me. Everything was so great today and still, the first time I left her alone, she ran.

Sitting in my office chair, I watch the video of the living room camera that goes to the front door. Not long after my meeting would have started I spot Jimmy walking into my house, which is odd, because my staff are not allowed in my house without me giving them permission. There's no fucking way I would have when I wasn't around. I did when she was chained in the basement, only because somebody had to be there to give her the food she refused. A few moments later another man comes in, but I don't recognize him. Why the fuck is he in my house? He speaks to Athena. I click on another camera, after making note of the time. I need to see her face. When I do, my blood turns to ice. I may not know who this man is, but my Butterfly does. Pure terror shows on her face. I intentionally have no sound on these devices, because if the feds come with a warrant, the things they'd hear could land me in prison for the rest of my life, and likely all the men in our family as well. Right now, I regret that, as I watch my wife get to her feet. She goes to put her shoes on, but the older man says something to her and she walks toward him. He grabs her by the back of her neck, squeezing hard, and I see fucking red. They walk out and I switch to the outside camera. She glances back at the house, and it looks like she's staring straight into my soul. The anguish on her face is not something I'll soon forget. It's going to haunt me.

She turns away, and gets into the white vehicle that has farm use plates on it. The man hands Jimmy a stack of cash, and gets in and drives away with my wife inside.

Picking up my whiskey decanter, I throw it across the room and it shatters near my desk, but I ignore it.

"Fuck!"

Whoever this asshole is, he has my wife, and that means he's a fucking dead man. And Jimmy is involved, obviously. He took money from the old man, so clearly he was paid off. That's the very reason I'll begin with him. *Wherever you are, Butterfly. I'll find you.* If I have to kill a billion men in the process, I don't mind. He took the one thing that is most precious to me, and for that he will fucking suffer.

I run a hand through my hair as I call each of my brothers, ordering them to get to the warehouse immediately. "Why the warehouse?" Kage was the first, but not the last, to ask. Normally I'd take Jimmy to the basement to question him, but the thought of going down there with so many memories of my wife, is more than I can bear. Fuck. I miss her.

Walking outside, I find Jimmy standing near the guard station with Eduardo. I call Stephen to take over their post, while I question both of them. While I didn't see Eduardo on the video like I did Jimmy, those two are thick as thieves, and if one is involved the other one probably is too.

"Hand me your weapons."

This is a skill I learned from my father. Always appear composed. Never let them see you break. Right now it's a struggle, but I still pull it off.

They exchange worried glances, before Jimmy says, "Boss. What's going on?"

Some people would say I'm crazy to approach two armed men like this. I am carrying, I always am, but my gun is not in my hand. As my dad would say, 'there's more than one way to skin a cat.' I don't need a weapon to kill either of them, and it would be stupid for them to pull a gun on me. They both know me well, and are aware that I could have them screaming in pain from the floor, long before they managed to fire a shot. They both hand me their .45s, and I tuck them both into the back of my waistband. There are other weapons in the guard shack, but they normally only wear one in their holsters.

"Come on. We're going to have a chat. Warehouse. You'll both walk in front of me, so I can keep my eyes on you." Eduardo looks at me with fear. He has only just figured out they are in very big trouble. Maybe he is innocent, because Jimmy reeked of guilt the moment I approached them. Time will tell, I suppose.

Once we get to the large warehouse, I nod to Eduardo. "Go on. You know the code. I have trusted you for how long?"

He enters the code, and answers me, "Twenty-two years, Boss. And before that I worked for your father."

We all walk inside and they turn to me, waiting for an order.

"Down to your underwear."

129

Jimmy stares at me like I've lost my mind. "What?"

"Strip now. I don't feel like patting you down, to be sure you don't have any other weapons hidden."

Eduardo is the first to comply, probably because he has known me the longest. He knows if someone refuses an order, how that turns out for them. Not well. I expect my men to do as they're told, no matter what. I pay them well. They are treated with respect. I've written checks to Eduardo's daughter's private school since she was six years old. That wasn't part of his pay, it was extra, because I don't want my men to struggle financially. People who fail to make ends meet do stupid fucking things. This is my way of preventing that. My foot soldiers never worry about that shit. They know if they come to me with a problem, I'll find a way to fix it. I'm a good boss. Yet when someone fucks with myself, or my family, that all evaporates in the blink of an eye. They will be treated in a hostile manner like any other enemy.

"Kneel."

Both men get to their knees, both of them wearing a fearful expression.

"Jimmy, let's start with you. I have reviewed the camera footage from earlier today. I want to know who the fuck the man was that you let into my house. The same one who handed you a stack of cash. And WHERE THE FUCK IS MY WIFE?"

My voice booms in the empty warehouse, and the shock in Eduardo's eyes tells me he knows nothing about this. Until I find my wife, he is not going anywhere though.

I crack my knuckles, getting the attention of both of my men. They know what happens next.

"She isn't what you think she is," Jimmy says, with disgust dripping from his tongue.

I fold my arms over my chest. "Enlighten me."

Without turning around, I know my brothers are here. Reaper starts chuckling when he sees my men on their knees, wearing nothing except white cotton briefs.

"Tell me I get to kill someone," he says in a sick voice that would give a normal person chills down their spine. I glance over at him, and Kage puts his hand on his shoulder. "Down, boy. Bones wants information first."

Psycho walks over to Jimmy, and pets his hair as he stares down at him. "Did you do something bad, Jimmy?"

Jesus Christ. Obviously, I should've called Kage, and left the other two murderous lunatics out of this.

"Jimmy was going to inform me on the reasons why he says my wife is not what I think she is."

Psycho yanks his head back by a tight grip of his dark hair. "It's not polite to not look at someone when they're talking to you. Now speak."

His bottom lip trembles before he speaks. "I bet she didn't tell you about her special relationship with her father."

I glare at him. "Tell me what the fuck you know. Stop with the games."

"Her dad fucks her and she likes it. Disgusting, isn't it?"

The pain in my chest feels like it could swallow me whole. Who does this to their own child? Poor Athena. Is this true? Is this why my Butterfly is so guarded?

"How did you come to get this information?"

"Let me go, and I'll tell you everything."

All three of my brothers laugh in unison, because anybody that knows me knows there will be no walking away from this. With my wife being taken from me, it only cements that fact.

"You're not going anywhere, now spill."

"I needed money, so I took another job. He was looking for his missing daughter. Princess, he called her, was everything to him."

That's what Manny called her.

131

He shrugs his shoulders like it's no big deal, until Psycho pulls his hair so hard, he squeals like a stuck pig.

"When I told him I knew where she was, he offered me half a million dollars. I couldn't refuse it, because my little brother is in trouble with the law."

I shake my head, because had he come to me and asked for help, I would have given it to him. Now he's going to die. And who knows what will happen to his brother?

"Where is she?"

Jimmy glares at me. "Probably at his house in New Haven, Connecticut."

"Address, Jimmy."

He doesn't reply until Psycho pulls out his knife and holds it to his throat, then suddenly he wants to answer, "1604 Brighton Avenue."

"Psycho, let him go."

My brother immediately lets him go, and he coughs as he gasps for air. But we aren't done.

"Reaper, have at it. Make it quick. We're going to get my wife."

With a kick to his face, he falls onto his back screaming, and I feel regretful. I wish we had more time, it's sad really.

Reaper grabs his throat and squeezes hard, and looks down at him. I've seen this show before, but I've never enjoyed it as much as I do right now.

"The eyes are the window to the soul. Open your eyes. There's nothing more beautiful than watching a life leave its body. Don't cry, it only blurs the beauty. Do you see Jesus yet?"

He chuckles softly, and it's clear that my brother enjoys every second of this.

"Tell him pure evil said hi."

Releasing his grip on his throat, he checks his pulse. "He's dead."

I glance at Eduardo. "Kage, chain him up."

He goes out to his truck and comes back with chains, and secures Eduardo to a pillar. I gaze at Eduardo, who looks like he's trying to process everything that has happened.

"I didn't know."

I nod. "I mostly believe you. For now, you'll stay put. If you manage to get free and escape, I will kill you. Your innocence won't matter."

He shakes his head. "I understand, Boss. I'll be here when you return, and for what it's worth, I hope you find her and I hope she's okay. Even though Mrs. Bonetti shot me, she's a good woman, and doesn't deserve the things Jimmy said."

Chapter Twenty-Five

BONES

I toss my keys to Kage. "I need you to drive."

We all walk out to my Range Rover, and I climb into the back with Reaper beside me. Psycho sits in the front beside Kage. After setting up the GPS with directions, Kage takes off. Two hours and forty-nine minutes. Fuck. I would take the plane, but I'm afraid that would end up taking longer, so we have to drive.

"You alright?" Reaper asks with his hand on my shoulder.

I shake my head and admit, "No. If he has hurt her, I'll kill him, and never forgive myself."

He chuckles. "You're going to kill him anyway."

My brother isn't wrong. Simply taking her from me is reason enough. If he hurt her, the pain he experiences will be doled out with an intensity he could never imagine in his worst nightmares.

"Do you blame me?"

He grins like he's lost in a fantasy. "No. If it were my girl, I'd kill him and bring him back to life, a hundred times."

"Your girl?"

He laughs to himself. "Living dead girl. She's mine."

I scratch my head in confusion. "You tried to kill her, she ran, and now she's yours?"

Leaning back in his seat, he sighs. "She doesn't know it yet, but she will."

I laugh loudly, which is amazing in this situation, and Kage glances at me in the mirror and I say, "Serial killer is now a stalker apparently."

"Are you peeping in her windows?" Kage asks with a laugh.

Reaper snort laughs. "I'm not that much of a novice."

Poor living dead girl is in big trouble. My brother is nuts, and enjoys giving pain in a way the rest of us don't. I don't know what she did to catch his attention, but she's in for a dangerous ride.

"What's the plan, Bones?" Kage asks from the driver's seat.

I shrug, because I don't have a plan. We won't know until we get there exactly what needs to happen. Obviously, I'm killing her father, but the rest is very much up in the air.

"That depends on the shape I find my wife in. Just so we are crystal fucking clear, nobody looks at my wife."

Psycho chuckles beside Kage. "Bones is in loooove."

I grab the pen out of my jacket pocket, and chuck it at the back of his head. "Shut up, asshole. If you can't control your eyes, you can wait in the goddamn car."

He grumbles as he rubs the back of his head, "I get enough pussy, I don't need to look at yours."

Reaper turns to me. "Can I kill him?"

I shake my head. "Not a fucking chance, brother. He's all mine, but I might let you bring him back a few times."

My youngest brother may not be great at body disposal, but he has gifts. It's a shame my father threw him out of the business, because he could be useful. He will never be like the three of us and handle multiple things. He's hyper focused on one thing, and one thing only, but if we have him only handling that side of things, he could be an asset. I make a mental note to discuss it with my father. Our family has our hands in nearly all things illegal. We even own a few brothels, but we aren't involved in human trafficking. There are families that get into that shit, but we don't. Drugs, prostitution, weapons, everything else we do. We don't kill people every day, but it is often enough that Reaper might be able to satisfy his urges.

Kage pulls up to an area covered in trees, out in the middle of nowhere, with only wildlife.

"We are a mile away from the house, I assume you want to be sure he doesn't see you coming."

I nod my agreement, because with Athena there, I don't want to risk her safety. If she weren't there, I wouldn't fucking care.

All three of us are armed with several weapons, but they won't be used unless it's absolutely necessary. I have no intention of making this quick. My brothers know this about me, I don't have to say a word, but they also know if it's required to save my wife, I'll deal with it. Her safety is of the utmost importance. Everything else is secondary.

We approach the farmhouse and I glance around, taking in my surroundings. It's dark, but I can see well enough to spot the overgrown grass. The farmhouse is a dingy white, like someone hasn't taken care of this property in a long time. There's a fenced area off to the left, suggesting he might have cattle.

Reaper stares in the same direction. "I wonder if he has pigs."

I shake my head. "Let's go."

Kage looks to me for direction, and I respond. "Back."

We walk around to the back, and Psycho grabs tools out of his pocket and picks the lock. It would be easy to break the door down, but we're trying to get inside quietly. He holds the door open and I walk inside first, with my brothers following behind me. The first room we enter is a kitchen, with broken down cabinets, an old green stove and refrigerator, and stained cheap countertops. I wonder if he actually lives here as we walk through a long hallway. There's a living room off to the left, with a worn couch and sitting chair. The house appears to be empty, and I become concerned that she isn't here. I suddenly regret having Reaper kill Jimmy, because what if she's not here? I wasn't thinking clearly, and acted more like Psycho than myself.

Kage points to a door and whispers. "Basement?"

I nod as he opens the door, and I walk down the steps and pull the cord on the ceiling, that lights up the dark basement. It's an unfinished basement, with a soiled mattress on one side and that's it. Otherwise it's completely empty. And my wife is not here. Fuck.

We go back upstairs and check the bedrooms, but there's nobody here. Wherever he has her, it obviously isn't here. The panic surges through my blood, and I feel something I never feel. Fear. What if he killed her? Even thinking I'll never see her again makes it difficult to breathe.

"What the fuck is that?" Psycho asks, as he stares down the dimly lit hallway. It's not easy to see in here, and we didn't turn the lights on up here because we didn't want to give him a heads up, if he were here. The moonlight shines through a window, and causes a ring to almost glow. As I step closer, I realize it's a ring attached to a string so dingy it's nearly black. Psycho pulls it, and stairs come down from the attic. My heart pounds furiously as I walk up the steps. Several different scenarios run through my mind, as my breathing becomes heavy. None of them are the outcome I'm hoping for. I step over a black whip as I enter the room. Psycho hits a light switch and my heart shatters. Like the weak man I am for her, I fall to my knees as the blood pounds in my ears and cry out, "Butterfly."

My wife sits in the corner of a cage shivering, and it's not from the cold, because it's hot as hell up here. She's naked, and has lash marks on her body, and a swollen face. I notice the welts on her cheekbones, and physically feel her pain. What did he do to her? What kind of a father does this?

I move over to the cage and open it. "Butterfly, come here, baby."

My wife doesn't respond, she doesn't even look in my direction. It's as if she's gone. The dried tears on her face don't please me this time, they gut me.

Psycho breaks through my internal struggle. "We need wire cutters. I don't think she's going to come out on her own."

Still I have to try, because I don't have fucking wire cutters on me. None of us do.

"Butterfly. I love you. Please come to me, so I can make everything better."

She lifts her head and gazes at me, before she breaks me. "Leave me here to die, Luca."

"Fuck this."

I glance at Psycho. "If I can break bones, maybe I can break metal enough to go in and get her."

This cage is fucking old, so I'm hoping it has some weak points. It's not lost on me that this is the exact reason she's so terrified of being in a fucking cage. If she had told me, I probably would've still locked her in one initially, but the day I chained her never would've happened. Now I know the guilt is going to eat me alive, until there's nothing left but the shell of a man.

Athena watches as I attempt to break the cage apart on one side, and Psycho does the same on the other. It's too small of an opening, and if I attempt to get in, I'll be stuck in there with her, and I can't save her that way.

I look into her observing eyes. "I'm not leaving you here to die at his hands, Butterfly. Nobody hurts my wife like this and survives."

"Luca," she cries, and my heart feels like it's cracked open and bleeding.

"Butterfly, I'm here. Please come closer so I can keep you safe."

Her lashes flutter as her eyes connect with mine, and she whispers, "I told you, I don't like the cage."

I squat at the door to the cage. "I know, baby. I know, and after today I swear to you, you'll never be in another one."

Slowly she crawls to me, as she glances around at my brothers, like she's noticing them for the first time. I know she's probably feeling weird because she's naked, but I also know they aren't looking at her. Removing my jacket, I tell her, "Come here and put this on."

Her eyes widen, as if she has just realized she's naked, and she sits up and covers her breasts.

"Come here, Butterfly. I promise you nobody is looking at your body right now, myself included."

She makes the last few movements, until she's finally close enough to touch. Gently, I pull her out by putting my hands under her arms, and then put the jacket on her.

"Luca," she whispers, and I pull her into my arms, holding onto her for dear life.

"I'm here, baby."

Athena grips my shirt in both hands, and sobs into my chest. I lift her into my arms and make my way to the exit, and climb down the steps carefully.

Chapter Twenty-Six

ATHENA

He tries to sit me on the couch, but I wrap my arms around him, because right now I need him. I am terrified he'll leave me alone, and my father will find me. At first I wanted him to leave me to die, but I don't really want to die. Not this way.

Luca sits on the couch, with me in his arms. "It was your father who hit you?"

"Yes," I answer quietly because I know what question is coming.

Stroking my hair, he speaks quietly, maybe so his brothers don't hear him, "Did he rape you?"

The tears come instantly, and he gently kisses my swollen face. "It's okay, Butterfly, I just need to know."

I nod slightly, causing more pain in my head. "Yes," I whisper, and then add, "Just my mouth."

Luca holds me close to his chest as I cry. "I'm sorry, I'm so sorry."

The fact that I didn't want it doesn't mean I didn't cheat on my husband. Now that he knows, I don't expect him to stick around long term. Not only being with another man, but with my own father, is as disgusting as it gets. How do you even look at someone after knowing that information? I heard him when he said he loved me, but love only goes so far. You can love someone and not be able to stay with them. My mother loved my father desperately, and yet she left. Love does not make a marriage work.

"You have nothing to be sorry for. You did nothing wrong. He did, and I promise you, he'll pay for it with his life."

I warn him, "He might have a gun."

He chuckles softly. "And he won't ever get a chance to fire it."

I watch him as he orders his brothers around, and instantly understand why his dad wants to leave him in charge. "Psycho, go wait behind the back door, but don't approach him."

"Reaper, hallway."

Then he gives the final instruction, "Kage, go to the front door. I want no chance for him to make a run for it."

His three brothers don't argue or hesitate, they immediately move to wait where he told them to.

"Where are you going?"

He chuckles and leans down, kissing the top of my head. "Nowhere, Butterfly. Even while I'm making him cry, my eyes will always be on you."

Luca buttons up his jacket I'm wearing. "Where's your dress?"

I'm afraid to give him too much information, I don't want him to have detailed images in his mind, so I just say, "He wiped his face with it, and took it with him when he left. I don't know what he did with it, but I don't want it."

He arches a brow and stares at me. "Why did he wipe his face on it, Butterfly?"

I shrug like I don't know, but Luca doesn't buy it. "Tell me."

Shutting my eyes tight so I can't see his expression, I tell him the truth, "I spit his cum in his face."

He wraps his arms around me tightly, but I feel his clenched fists against my back. "You did good, wife. So good."

It doesn't feel good. None of this does. I'm glad he's going to kill him so he can't hurt other girls, while I don't know about it, somehow I know there's been others. Probably while I've been gone, for sure, but it doesn't take any of it away. It won't undo the damage, but at least I'll know he won't come after me again.

We sit quietly for what feels like hours, and we both perk up when we notice lights traveling across the windows.

"Do we need to-"

He presses his finger to my lips and whispers, "They know. My brothers don't miss much. I need you to sit beside me."

I nod silently and climb off his lap, and sit on the couch beside him.

Glancing at him, I see the violent smirk on his face, as he cracks his knuckles. The sound of the door echoes through the house, as do my father's footsteps. Holding my hand over my mouth, I try to stay quiet, but my heart is pounding. I'm afraid for me, and terrified he has a gun, and will fire it at Luca and his brothers, quicker than my husband expects. He walks past the living room entry and then suddenly stops. His footsteps get closer as he stares at me with rage. He flips the light switch on the wall and spots Luca.

As I expected, he pulls out a gun and points it directly at me, and then moves it to my would be savior. "I guarantee you, her pussy is not worth all this trouble. I would know, I had her first."

I can audibly hear Luca clenching his jaw, but he doesn't move.

Two of his brothers come up behind my father and grab his arms, pulling them back, and a gunshot goes off, hitting the wall as my heart stops.

"Reaper, Psycho; bring him in."

He drags his feet as they pull him, as if he knows who they are, and realizes how much trouble he is in. I try to draw a breath in as they bring him in front of us, and Luca barks, "That's close enough. He doesn't get within touching distance of my wife."

Glaring at my father, he says, "On your knees."

My father glares right back. "Fuck you, asshole."

Reaper laughs, while Psycho winces and says, "Oh, that's gonna cost you. He really hates being called an asshole."

Psycho grins at Reaper and it's not a smile, it's sadistic, and he says, "Ready, lil bro? Let's help the old man to his knees."

I imagine they might hit him behind the knees, but they don't. Moving in front of him, they kick his kneecaps hard, as he cries out in pain and falls to his knees, hitting the hardwood floor with a thud.

143

Luca takes my hand in his. "Butterfly, I'm going to ask you some questions, and I need you to know you're safe. I will not be angry with you for your responses. I need to know the truth, so I can decide what to do with this man that calls himself your father. Can you do that for me? Answer my questions honestly?"

I nod, but don't take my eyes off my father. It's not because I want to look at him, I don't, but watching him means he can't catch me off guard, when he comes for me. He will come for me. Somehow he always does.

"When did he first touch you in a sexual manner?"

I swallow hard and admit, "Not long before my sixth birthday."

He kisses my hand. "Good girl. How many times did he lock you in a cage?"

My head snaps to Luca's gaze, as I look at him like he must know, and realize he doesn't.

"More often than not."

Luca scratches his head with his free hand. "Okay, I need to know more than that. Out of seven days, how many, do you think?"

"Seven."

He glances at his brother Kage and then back to me. "Tell me how a normal day would go. You went to school, came home, and then you went back in? Or you were out for a little while? I'm trying to figure out how much this cage factors into things."

I shake my head and then lower it, as the shame fills me. "I didn't go to school, Luca. It was always me in the cage, unless he took me out to use me."

Glancing up, I watch him turn white as a ghost, and I know it's over. The way he looks at me now, with nothing but pity.

He squeezes my hand. "And he hit you?"

I nod. "Yes."

Kissing my hand again, he sets it on my lap. "Good girl. Thank you. Please stay sitting right here, Butterfly. Don't move unless you're told to."

"Okay," I whisper as he rises off the couch, and walks over to my father.

When he speaks, his voice comes out low and threatening, and a shiver works its way down my spine. "I must apologize, I'm a little out of my element here. Under normal circumstances, I know how much pain fits the crime of the person kneeling before me, but your crimes are so heinous, I don't know where to begin."

My father glances up into his face, and attempts to sound strong, but his voice is shaky and weak. "Get on with it, asshole."

Luca smirks at him. "Very well. How does an appetizer of a dislocated shoulder sound?"

He doesn't respond to him, and instead he looks at me. "You're a worthless cunt, and he will realize that. How many times while he's fucking you, will he wonder what it sounded like when you screamed daddy?"

Psycho moves behind him, grabs him by his hair and pulls his head back, kneeing him in the face, as he growls, "Don't fucking talk to my sister-in-law."

My father screams in pain as blood pours from his face. It's hard to see whether it's coming from his nose or mouth.

Luca chuckles. "Okay, broken nose and *then* a dislocated shoulder."

He lifts his leg and puts his foot on his shoulder, as Kage lifts his arm and Luca takes it, and swiftly pulls it back and up, while slamming his foot down.

His screams echo through the room while I watch, and feel like there's something wrong with me. I shouldn't like this, but I do.

"Oops. I didn't mean to break your arm. Yet."

I sit forward on the couch, watching every movement, enjoying every scream from my father and Luca grins at me. "Does he have a tool bag?"

Shrugging, I say, "I don't know, but when I was little, he kept it on the top shelf in the bedroom closet."

Psycho whistles as he leaves the room, and a few minutes later comes back with a black bag in his hands.

"Any bolt cutters in there? I have a fun idea."

Chapter Twenty-Seven
BONES

"Take his clothing off."

All three of my brothers groan. "Come on," Psycho complains.

I narrow my gaze at him. "He needs to be castrated."

Glancing at my wife, I ask, "If you want to get revenge, now would be the time."

She shakes her head, but I can see the obvious interest in her eyes.

"It's up to you, but my brothers will hold his arms behind his back while he screams. He will never touch you."

Athena nods her head. "Okay. I'll try."

When I say my wife is fucking gorgeous, I mean it. No woman should look as beautiful as she does, even with the swelling on her face, a black eye, and a purple bruise on her cheekbone.

Psycho hands me the bolt cutters and I take them. He and Reaper grab his arms, and pull back as he screams in pain.

"Stand on his legs."

Both of my brothers put a foot on the back of his calves, holding him in place.

"Kage, pull his pants down."

He groans, "Fucking hell," but he does as I asked and pops the button open, and yanks his pants down, exposing his little dick.

I show Athena the bolt cutters and motion her over to me. She rises off the couch and walks over to me slowly, nervously.

"You just need to open them, put them on his little dick or balls, whichever you prefer, then close them and they will cut through the skin."

The truth is I've never done this, but I'm sure if they can cut through a bolt, they'll be able to cut through skin. And it doesn't matter if she actually detaches it. It's about the pain, he's not going to be alive to use his pathetic dick anyway.

She takes the bolt cutters in her shaky hands.

"Butterfly, are you okay? You don't have to do this if you don't want to."

Her lashes flutter as her gaze lifts to mine. "I've been dreaming about something like this since I was a girl. I want this. No, I need this."

My wife is sexy as hell, but I've never seen her sexier than she is right now. Athena looks like a fucking vengeful goddess as she holds the bolt cutters in her hand, and her lips pull into a slight smile.

She glares at her father. "Every time you made me open my mouth for you, you destroyed a part of me. When you put your little dick inside me, where it never belonged, you took even more. You caged me like an animal. Denied me the opportunity for an education. Now you'll pay the price for doing those things to me with your life, but not before you suffer incredible pain. My husband is a real man, unlike you, and he will make sure your agony is great."

My wife smiles at her abuser with the biggest smile I've seen on her face. "This is going to hurt."

I nod to my brother. "Hold his head back, and make him look at her."

Psycho grabs the back of his head and forces it back. He stares at my wife with wide eyes, and a tear runs down his cheek as he trembles.

Reaper puts his fingers on his eyelids and pulls up. "Keep your eyes open while she cuts your tiny dick off. If you close them, I'll cut them out. I have a thing for eyes."

I shake my head, because my little brother gives me a headache sometimes, even though his words were truthful, and I have no doubt he will cut the man's eyes out if he doesn't comply.

Athena holds the open bolt cutters and wedges them around his dick. "Wow, this wouldn't work if you had a big dick."

148

I smirk at her. "Remember that, Butterfly."

"I just squeeze the handles together?"

I'm careful not to touch her because I don't want to spook her, causing her to get hurt, but fuck, I want to.

"Yes, squeeze it as tight as you can. Oh and expect blood."

How much blood I don't really know, but there's got to be some. I have never in my life cut off a man's junk. Ever. Normally I break bones, slice the occasional throat, but never this. Yet, nothing seems more fitting than this right here.

Athena squeezes, and lets out an evil laugh as he screams. It's a sound I've never in my life heard, and I'm quite used to the sounds of pain. Any man ever kicked in the nuts can verify how bad it hurts, and I have no doubt that it's pure agony. Watching my brothers wince as she does it causes me to laugh louder than I mean to.

Blood squirts from his dickless body, and Athena stares with a fascinated expression. "His dick fell off."

I take the tool from her hand. "You did so well, Butterfly. Go sit on the couch. I don't want you to get hurt."

"Hold on, Luca. Don't rush me."

Glancing at her, I'm confused when she asks, "Does anybody have a glove?"

Reaper pulls a glove out of his back pocket and hands it to her. She puts it on her right hand and glances at me. "His disgusting penis has touched my skin for the last time."

I watch her with curiosity as she bends down and picks up the severed member, and stands in front of him. "Open wide, Princess."

He shakes his head no, but when my brother pulls out his knife and digs the tip into his eye, he opens his mouth to scream, and my wife shoves his dick into his mouth. I don't have a weak stomach, but listening to him gag on his own dick is a little gross.

"Tape?"

Psycho says, "Oh, I saw some in the bag."

Since he's still holding his head, so he's forced to look at my wife while she literally destroys his manhood, Kage goes into the bag and grabs the duct tape. He tears a piece off and hands it to Athena, who promptly takes it and tapes his mouth shut.

Jesus Christ, this woman is fucking incredible. My wife is a natural born killer.

She gazes at me sweetly, and it takes everything in me to not slam my lips to hers. I want to, fucking desperately, but after what she's been through, I don't. I'm generally a selfish bastard that takes what I want, when I want it, but this is my wife, the mother of my future children, and the more I've learned about her life before me, the more I realize she probably isn't okay. A daughter of a friend of my father's was trafficked years ago, and treated a lot like Athena was. After years of abuse, she was rescued. She spent three years in and out of psychiatric facilities, before she ultimately took her own life. I'm terrified of something like that happening with my wife. Right now she's putting on a brave face, and showing nothing but strength, but I fear when she's alone, the demons will haunt her.

I watch Athena move to the couch and take a seat, before turning my attention back to her father.

Glaring at him, I smile. "You'll forgive us if we are taking too long to decide how to kill you. We're all brothers, but tend to kill differently. Psycho here would love nothing more than to slash your throat, and watch the blood pour from you. Reaper would choke you, but then you're already choking on your own dick, aren't you? I would break your bones, and Kage? Well, he would lock you in a cage, and leave you until you starve to death. So you see, there are a lot of options."

Tipping his head back, he takes all of our options away, but it's fitting. He attempts to cough as the dick appears to lodge in his throat, cutting off his air supply, and his face turns red while he visibly freaks out from the lack of air. He tries to move, but with my brothers holding him in place, he can't. I glance at my watch,

150

because I wonder how long it takes someone to choke to death on their own cock. My eyes move from him to my watch, as I wait for my answer. Seven minutes and eight seconds.

I would have preferred to cause him more pain, but this works, because the very thing he used to torment my wife is how he died.

My brothers drop his body to the floor, and I watch as Athena gets up and walks out of the room.

I have no idea where she's going. Could she have something she wants here? I don't know if this is her childhood home. I follow behind her, but at a distance, because I want to see what she's doing. She takes the first few steps up to the attic, so I calmly say her name, "Athena."

Continuing to follow her, I don't understand why the hell she'd want to go back up there for anything.

When I make it to the top and step into the attic, I find her kneeling in front of her metal nightmare. Her breathing is heavy and audible, as I step closer to her and kneel beside her.

"I don't like to be kept in a cage," she whispers, and I think it's more to herself than to me. Stroking her hair, I tell her, "I know, Butterfly and that's over now. Never again."

A tear rolls down her cheek while she runs her fingers down the cage. "I don't know what to do with my life now. At twenty-four, I should know."

My arms ache to hold her, but I hold myself back. "Whatever you want to do. As long as your plans involve me, there are no limits."

She laughs, but it's not genuine, it's bitter. "It's not so simple, Luca. I can't even order food in a restaurant, because I can't read the menu. And you want me to have your children? Don't you think they deserve better than this?"

I lose all the fight I had in me to do the right thing, and not touch her much without her wanting it. I'm a selfish bastard, so I pull her into my arms. "You deserved better than this, wife. So much fucking better. And you will have it. I swear to you, we're going to undo

151

everything he did. You will learn to read. You will get an education. Nothing is out of reach for you, Butterfly."

Chapter Twenty-Eight

ATHENA

I don't understand my emotions at all. Luca should terrify me, and I still can't comprehend why he feels like safety to me. He has not hurt me as much as my father did, I'm not sure that would be possible, but he has done bad things to me. Yet, right now none of that seems to matter, as I clutch onto him like I'm falling from the edge of a cliff, and he's the only one that can save me from certain death.

One of his brothers comes up behind us, I'm not sure who it is, because they all sound so alike. "The cleaners will be here in half an hour, we need to go."

I glance at Luca with confusion. "Like a maid?"

He chuckles softly. "Not exactly, Butterfly. Are you ready to go home now?"

Trembling in his arms, I admit, "I can't go back there, Luca. Please don't make me."

"Why?" he asks, looking at me with confusion.

Placing his hand on my chin, he tilts my head back gently, and looking into my eyes with concern, he says, "Why, Butterfly? You need to talk to me."

"Jimmy."

He leans his head down and presses his lips to mine, and kisses me softly. "Nobody who has anything to do with my wife being hurt, lives. Including my own fucking men. Jimmy is gone."

Rising to his feet, he lifts me into his arms. "We are going home, and having a doctor look at your injuries."

Shaking my head, I say, "I'm fine."

He groans slightly. "Beautiful wife, this is not open for discussion. There will be no argument. I will make sure you're okay."

I don't fight him any further, because my entire face throbs with pain. Maybe the doctor can give me something to ease it. Wrapping my arms around his neck, I press my face to his chest and inhale his comforting scent.

"It's a long walk to the car, but I'm carrying you."

We walk out of the house and the cool fresh air hits me in the face. I breathe it in, and it's so wonderful, I start to cry.

"What's wrong?"

I laugh through my tears, because I know it's ridiculous, but I tell him the truth, "When he brought me back here, I thought it was over, honestly, I never expected to see outside ever again."

Luca kisses me on the top of the head. "Tomorrow, I'll show you the outside of the house. I think you're going to enjoy it, and you can spend as much time out there as you'd like."

"Do you have a swimming pool? My mom used to tell me about this pool she went to as a teenager. It sounded like fun."

He stops walking and stares at me. "Yeah, Butterfly, I have a pool. In fact I have two, but you need to learn to swim before using them alone. Jesus, baby, your life is going to change."

Does he think I've never seen a pool before? I've never been in one, but there was one at the hotel Manny kept me at. I wasn't allowed to go outside much unless I was doing a job, but I used to stare out the window during the day, and watch the children play in the water. To this day, I think about the one little girl I saw. Her hair was dark, almost the identical shade of mine, and she had the cutest smile when she laughed. She splashed her mother with water, and would break out into a fit of giggles. It was the way she looked at her mom, and the way her mother gazed at her in return. It wasn't just love, but absolute adoration, and I wondered what that would be like. I bet that little girl's mom would not have left her with a monster.

Reaper races up to us. "Here. I found this."

Luca takes the blanket and covers me with it, before adjusting his hands around me, over the material I remember well. It was my mom's, and I was always surprised she didn't take her great grandmother's blanket with her when she left.

He lowers me into the backseat of the car, and gets in beside me, before pulling me onto his lap. Psycho and Kage get into the front, while Reaper gets into the back beside Luca. Leaning his head down, Luca kisses the bruises on my face softly. "Butterfly." His voice sounds strained and thick with emotion. He doesn't say anything further, instead he holds me close like I'm precious cargo that he can't bear to let go of.

I wake to soft kisses on my neck. "We're home, baby."

My eyes flutter open, as my heart pounds and I clutch his shirt, while the realization dawns on me that I'm in Luca's arms.

"Shhh, it's okay. I'm here, nothing bad is going to happen. It's over."

His deep voice calms me in an instant. I should laugh at myself, because there is no way *this man* should have this ability. This power over me. Instead of holding onto him, I should be running for the hills, but I won't, because where the hell would I even go? The truth is even if I had somewhere to go, I'd miss him. My husband has forced his will over me more than once. The same man that breaks bones as a hobby. While it doesn't make any sense, I hold him tighter and bury my face in his chest, inhaling that spicy orange scent that seems to chase everything bad away.

Luca slides out of the car, and leans in and lifts me into his arms again. "I can walk."

He chuckles softly, as he holds me against his chest with my legs over one of his arms. "I think I like this, Butterfly. I might start carrying you everywhere."

I attempt to roll my eyes at him and pain shoots through my right eye, causing me to close my eyes, and wince from pain.

"And you didn't want to see the doctor. Stubborn girl."

Wrapping my arms around his neck, I press my face against his chest, as the throbbing seems to keep getting worse.

He carries me into the house and upstairs to the bedroom, and after sitting me on the bed, he narrows his gaze at me. "Stay. I'm getting you a bathrobe. The doctor will be here any minute, and I don't want him to see my wife naked."

"He?" I panic slightly as Luca heads to the bathroom. Bringing me the white fluffy robe, I remove his jacket and put it on, and repeat myself, "He?"

Sitting on the bed while I get changed, I can tell he's intentionally not allowing himself to gaze at my naked body, and I wonder if that's how it will be now. Finding out your wife sucked her father's dick is likely not fun. Am I bitter? Maybe a little. Underneath the fact that I never wanted him to touch me that way, lies the embarrassment. Pure humiliation. I wanted someone to save me, but not my husband. How will he ever look at me with anything other than disgust again? It's going to be like William all over again. Luca will look at me like I'm dirty. Unwashable. Eventually he'll stop trying to look at me at all. Will he stay married to me, even though he can't bear to touch me? Or will he throw me away like the trash I am? He may not be a good man, but a man like Luca Bonetti has women throwing themselves at his feet. I've not witnessed it, but I know it's true. He is many things, but hard to look at is not one of them.

Luca keeps his eyes on mine as I change, and I sit on the bed once I have the belt done up. With a sigh, he explains, "I'm sure a woman in your situation would prefer a female doctor. I promise I'll secure a woman for you to see regularly, but you cannot wait, Butterfly. I need to make sure you're okay. Doc Johnson is my personal doctor. He has a practice in Las Vegas, and I called him when I realized your father took you," he grits his teeth, "against your will. He flew out immediately. Please don't fight me on this."

With a nod, I take a deep breath. "Okay, but can you stay in the room? I don't want to be alone with him. You don't have to look at me, just make sure he doesn't hurt me."

"I don't have to look at you? What the fuck does that mean?"

Luckily we are interrupted by a knock at the door, and I'm not forced to answer that question.

"Come in," Luca growls, clearly irritated with me.

The older gentleman, with white hair and matching bushy eyebrows, enters the room and shakes Luca's hand. "Mr. Bonetti. Good to see you again, sir."

He smiles at me softly. "This must be the Mrs. Bonetti I've heard so much about."

My eyes dart between the two of them, and Luca instructs the doctor, "This is my wife. You'll be allowed to see what you need to, no more. She is not for your viewing pleasure. Tread carefully, Doc."

I would roll my eyes if it didn't hurt so much as the last time I did that. He's ridiculous.

"Understood. Shall we get started?"

He pulls a light out of his pocket. "Follow the light with your eyes please."

I do and he says, "Good. Now these bruises on your face, can you tell me how they happened?"

When I look at him with a confused expression, he clarifies, "What were you hit with?"

"My face? He hit me with his hand and his fist."

I try to ignore Luca's clenching fists, and focus on the doctor.

"Did he hit you somewhere else with something else?"

157

Before I can respond, my husband barks, "All over her upper body with a fucking whip."

The doctor arches an eyebrow. "May I take a look? I want to be sure there are no open wounds that may become infected."

Glancing at Luca, he nods his head, with a clenched jaw, and I lower the bathrobe, exposing my breasts to a man I've never met before. To his credit, he looks quickly and asks, "Any on the back?"

Turning around, I show him my back as well.

"Thank you, you may put the robe back on, young lady."

After I secure it, I rotate on the bed again until I am facing him.

"Did he penetrate you?"

I shake my head no. "Not there, no. Just my mouth."

He scratches his head and looks at Luca. "This man should be prosecuted to the fullest extent of the law, Mr. Bonetti, but knowing you there are no bones left to prosecute. She's going to be fine, physically speaking. The wounds are all superficial. I will give her medication for the next few days to help with the pain, but she shouldn't need it longer than that. What she does need is someone to talk to. I will give you the names of a few female therapists skilled in dealing with this type of trauma. It's crucial that you deal with not only the physical, but the emotional effects, of this kind of abuse."

Luca nods. "I assure you, I will schedule something tomorrow."

Chapter Twenty-Nine

Bones

The doctor leaves, and I watch Athena nervously messing with the tie on the robe. I'm not used to doing the right thing when it comes to women, but I'm trying with her.

"I should make you something to eat."

"I'm filthy, I need to take a shower and brush my teeth."

She doesn't appear dirty, so I assume she's referring to what that fucking piece of shit did to her.

"I'll start the water for your shower."

Walking into the bathroom, I turn the water on and after it's hot, I call to her, "Come on, baby. It's ready."

She comes in and drops her robe and steps into the shower.

"Are you coming in?"

Fuck, I want to, but I shouldn't.

I turn to walk out the door, and she speaks in a low, shaky voice, "If you're going to end this, can you just do it? I can't handle the suspense."

My head snaps around before my body has a chance to catch up. "What? I'm sure I misheard you."

She stares at the floor and speaks, this time barely above a whisper, "If you're going to end this, can you just do it?"

Walking over to her, I climb into the shower with my clothes on and take her hands in mine. "Butterfly, look at me."

She lifts her head, and gazes at me with watery eyes, and I ask, "Why the hell would I end this marriage?"

A tear rolls down her cheek. "Look at me, Luca. That's right, you can't. I repulse you and honestly, I don't blame you for it."

"What?"

I'm so fucking lost, I may as well be in complete darkness. I have no clue where any of this is coming from? End this? Everything that happened tonight was for her. How could she even suggest I'd walk away?

"I am looking at you right now, Athena."

She shakes her head in disagreement. "No, Luca. Since you found me, you haven't been able to look at my body. Tell me I'm a liar."

"Jesus Christ, Athena. I just rescued you from a cage. You were fucking naked. He raped you. Maybe he didn't touch your pussy, but he fucking raped you. I'm trying to be respectful. I'll admit, it's not something I'm used to, so maybe I'm doing it wrong. I have no issues with looking at your beautiful body and, when you're ready, I'll have no problem fucking it either. This marriage will not end. Not today, not tomorrow, and not fifteen fucking years from now. You're mine, and that has not changed."

I lean over her, and nearly lose my mind when her breathing picks up. Her chest rises and falls with heavy breaths, and it takes everything in me not to rip my clothes off, and give her a reason to breathe heavily.

"Do we understand each other?"

"Yes, Luca," she nearly pants.

If she were any other woman, I'd likely already be balls deep inside her. But she isn't any other woman. She's my goddamn wife, and has been through hell. I need her mentally stable when she has my children.

I have not had to jerk off in years, but staring at my beautiful woman, I know I will have to soon. The last thing I want to do is push her too soon, and cause more psychological damage.

"Tell me what you need from me."

"You."

I soap up my hands, and gently wash her skin as the tears roll down her cheeks.

"Tell me specifically what you need, Butterfly."

She closes her eyes like she's wincing from pain. "I need you to touch me. Hold me. And tell me everything is going to be okay, even if you yourself don't believe it."

Quickly, I rinse her body and get her out of the shower and into a clean fluffy robe, before stripping out of my drenched clothing.

When my wife asks me to touch her, I'll never hesitate. I stand beside her as she brushes her teeth, and pays special attention to her tongue. I know she wants to wash away what he did to her even though she can't. But I'll let her try. Whatever makes her feel better.

"All done," she sighs audibly, as she places her toothbrush back in the holder. I scoop her into my arms, and walk her over to the bed and lay her down, before climbing in beside her and pulling her into my arms. She's the perfect fit, like her body was made to be molded with mine. I'm fucking crazy about this woman. It was never part of the plan. Hell, I never even imagined I'd like her, but here we are. I would turn into a serial killer like my brother if I had to, in order to keep her safe.

Rolling onto my back, I pull her on top of me as she cries, with her face pressed to my neck.

"Go ahead and cry, Butterfly. Get it all out, but everything will be okay. We will get through this together and I swear to you, nothing like this will ever happen again."

"I'm so sorry," she sobs, "I didn't want it. I'm sorry."

Gently, I flip her over to her back, and stare into her wet eyes. "Of course you didn't. Do not fucking apologize for what he did to you."

She shakes her head. "We're married, Luca. It was wrong."

Jesus Christ, this woman makes me fucking feral for her.

I stroke my fingers down her cheek and, leaning forward, I lick her salty tears and groan. "Wife, we both know you had no choice. You didn't break any vows. I'm not angry with you. Stop blaming yourself for something you did not choose."

"Luca," she whispers, and that one little word is all it takes for me to lose my goddamn mind. I have never asked for permission with a woman. She's the only one that deserves it. After what she's been through, it feels necessary.

"Butterfly, please let me kiss you."

Darting her tongue out, she moistens her lips and says, "Please."

I press my lips to hers and slide my tongue into her mouth. As always, she tastes so fucking sweet. The fact that I could've lost her only increases my need for her. He could have easily killed my wife, before I even realized she was gone. I tilt my head, deepening our kiss, wanting so much more than I can take from her right now. I'm not a good man, the polar opposite, but for her I want to be.

I want her to crave me. Need me. And fall so in love with me she can't fucking see straight. I want her to be as obsessed with me as I am with her.

Pulling back from our kiss, I ask, "What do you want to eat?"

She shakes her head. "I'm not hungry. Just tired. I promise I'll eat tomorrow. Please, can I sleep?"

Rolling over onto my back, I pat my chest. "Come here, Butterfly. This is where you sleep."

With a small smile on her lips, one that makes my heart squeeze, she slips out of her robe and spreads her body semi prone over mine.

She breathes a contented sigh as I place my arms around her and hold her tight. Tomorrow I'll arrange therapy for her. I glance at the time on the wall, and notice that Stefan should be here soon with her medication, if he hasn't been already. He would leave it downstairs. He knows better than to come to my bedroom. Eduardo being in the warehouse, and my men knowing about it, will most certainly help them toe the line. Tomorrow I'll need to find out if he has ever crossed a line with my wife. I'm confident he wasn't involved in allowing her father to take her, so if he didn't do something I don't know about to earn his death, I'll set him free.

Athena falls asleep in my arms while I watch her. Even with the nasty bruising and swelling on her skin, she's so beautiful. The moment I saw her in that cage, it nearly broke me. Realization quickly came to me. Now, the day I left her chained in the basement while she cried my name haunts me. Had I known her history, I would've done things differently. Hell, had I known, I wouldn't have gone to Vegas. Instead, I would've been searching for her father and killing him. It would've prevented him from hurting her again. Yet, I can't be mad at her for not telling me. Why would she trust a man like me with that information?

After being asleep for less than an hour, she digs her nails into my chest and whimpers quietly.

"Shh, I'm here, Butterfly."

I rub her back gently, coaxing her back to sleep. Continuing to watch her, I think back to the day she had the gun on Eduardo. Jimmy had said she was going to shoot him unless they killed her. Is that what she wanted? To die?

Shifting slightly, I reach over and grab my cell phone off the nightstand, and see a text from my brother, Psycho.

Psycho: *I'm the oldest, asshole.*

I roll my eyes at his irritation. Yes, he is the oldest, and if he could be trusted, he would've been the head of the family when our father passes away.

Me: *Yes, you are. It wasn't my decision, but I don't disagree with it either.*

I knew he'd be pissed, so this isn't exactly a surprise. We were always raised with the expectation that he would one day take over the family. He is the reason he won't be. Chances are good that punches will be thrown, but it won't go beyond that. As angry as he might be, at the end of the day we are family. Two of my brothers are absolutely unhinged, but we are all close. I know without hesitation, all three of them will always have my back. Psycho will lash out, but if I need him, he'll be at my side.

Chapter Thirty

ATHENA

"Wake up, sleeping beauty."

I begin to stir, and feel soft kisses on my neck and open my eyes, blinking them quickly as I focus on Luca standing beside the bed. He leans over me, with a hand on either side of me on the mattress as he stares at me.

"You made me a promise. Time for you to deliver."

I groan from the pain in my face. "You also made me a promise."

His lips form a delicious smirk. "Did I? I don't remember that."

"Even more than something for this pain, I want to go outside."

He straightens up and grabs a glass of water from the bedside table. "Sit up."

I do, and he hands me the glass and two pills. "The medication the doctor prescribed."

Staring at the drugs in my hand, I hesitate.

"Butterfly, I won't hurt you, I promise. This is what he sent to the pharmacy. You can trust me, and you can trust Doc Johnson."

I nod, but then wince from the throbbing in my head and take them.

"Maybe I should bring you breakfast in bed."

"Luca, no!"

I jump up, because there's only one thing I want. It's hard to explain to someone that hasn't lived in captivity for most of their lives, but I try.

"The most healing thing I can do is to go outside. I'm sure you don't understand it, but the sun shining on my face, the warmth touching my skin, the open area. It's everything to me. It makes me feel normal."

He runs his knuckles down my cheek with one hand, while taking the glass from me with his other. "Alright, beautiful wife. Let's put your order in with the chef and we can eat outside, so we both get what we need."

I get up and grab clothing from the closet, and slip on a purple dress I haven't worn yet. Luca chuckles softly. "That got you to move."

"Why is me eating so important to you?"

He steps closer to me, and places his hand on the side of my neck, and speaks low, "You're mine, Butterfly. That means I need to take care of you, but not because I have to. I want to."

Luca leans in closer and I panic. "Don't kiss me."

He lifts an eyebrow in surprise, as I giggle and cover my mouth. "I need to brush my teeth."

Grabbing the back of my neck with one hand, and prying my hand from my face with the other, he closes the distance and slams his lips to mine. He groans as he forces his tongue into my mouth, and slides it against mine in a sloppy kiss, and pulls back with a chuckle.

"Such a sweet tasting dirty mouth."

"Luca," I whisper, while feeling my cheeks heat with embarrassment. Shaking my head, I turn away from him, and head into the bathroom to brush my teeth.

He stands in the doorway with his hands on the top of the frame, showing off every muscle in his upper body. Glancing at him, I scold him, "You don't have to watch me."

His eyes narrow at me, before he breaks out into a boyish grin. "Oh, but I like watching my wife. She's absolutely captivating."

I spit into the sink and shake my head, as I rinse my toothbrush off. "Yeah, these bruises are so pretty."

He clenches his jaw. "No. They aren't. Every time I look at them, I want to kill him all over again. If I had known, he would've never got his hands on you. I would have destroyed him before he came into my home and took my wife. Bruises or not. Black eye or not.

166

You are still the most stunning woman I've ever seen. No other woman holds a candle to you. Fucking gorgeous."

I walk closer to him and wrap my arms around his waist. "You're very sweet for an asshole," I say with a mischievous grin.

He growls as he returns my embrace, and leans down close to my ear. "Careful, Butterfly."

His breath is warm and fans over my ear, causing me to shiver.

"Fuck, baby, you make me crazy. Let's go, before I do something I'll hate myself for."

Luca takes my hand in his, and we walk out of the room, and down the stairs to a back door I didn't know existed.

"You can come out here whenever you want, but must have a guard with you at all times. And I don't want you in the pool unless I'm around, until you learn how to swim. I'll hire an instructor for you."

"I hope he's hot," I say with a smirk.

He chuckles. "*She* will be."

We step out into the warm sun and I gasp. If I thought the inside was nice, this is next level. I only saw part of the backyard when we got married. This is a completely different section. The entire area is covered with rock formations and waterfalls. In the center, there's a massive pool that's the bluest I've ever seen, with rocks on the far end and another waterfall flowing over them. Tropical looking plants are scattered throughout the area. This place is his back yard, but looks like a tropical oasis.

"Luca, this is amazing. How big is your property?"

Wrapping his arm around my waist, he pulls me tight against his side. "Our property, wife. What's mine is yours. Our property is three hundred twenty-nine acres, and almost all of it is accessible to you. Only the warehouse is off limits."

I glance up at him and ask, "Why? What happens there?"

He chuckles softly, as he tucks my hair behind my ear. "Nothing good, baby. You don't need to be in there. If you need me and I'm in there, one of my men will get me."

I nod and he asks, "What do you want to eat?"

"What are my options?"

Leaning his head down, he kisses me on the forehead. "Whatever my wife wants, she gets. Tell me what you want, and our chef will prepare it."

This is not something I'm used to. My father used to bring me breakfast and dinner. My morning meal was always oatmeal, which I hate, and I frequently wondered if that's why he brought it to me. Whereas Manny would never give me breakfast. I got dinner three times a week, and sometimes lunch. Only enough to keep me alive. And I never had much of a choice with either of them. Complaining meant violence.

"Baby?"

I shrug. "I don't know. I'm not used to choices."

"What's your favorite?"

I close my eyes and remember a more pleasant time. "When I was really little, my mom used to make me pancakes. And bacon."

The memory is distant but still there. We used to sit at the table outside for breakfast. The birds chirped as I shoveled syrupy goodness into my mouth. There was laughter, so much laughter. Things were mostly good and then she left.

I open my eyes and blink away the unshed tears. "Pancakes and bacon, please. If it's not too much trouble."

Luca kisses me softly on the lips. "If my wife wants it, she gets it. I don't give a fuck how much trouble it is. I promise you, our staff is paid well for their trouble."

He pulls out his cell phone and dials a number. I guess it's the chef when I hear his side of the conversation. "Mrs. Bonetti will have pancakes, bacon, and whatever extras you think of, because that's not enough. I'll have my usual, Teddy. And coffee."

Placing his phone back in his pocket, he takes my hand and we walk across a wooden bridge to a large patio, with a wrought-iron table with a purple umbrella covering it. Luca pulls out a chair for me, and I arch a suspicious eyebrow, but take a seat, anyway.

He chuckles as he moves to the chair on the other side of the table and takes a seat. "I can be nice to my wife."

I giggle as I push my hair out of my face. "It would appear so."

A server comes over with coffee and orange juice, and sets it in front of us, and immediately walks away.

"You live quite the privileged life, Mr. Bonetti."

He grins at me with a nod. "I do, and now so do you, but I work hard for every penny we have, wife."

"Breaking bones," I joke before I take a sip of my coffee, and he laughs out loud.

"Is that all you think I do?"

Licking my lips, I say, "This coffee is really good, but to answer your question, I saw a mafia movie once. So you probably do a lot of the shady shit I saw on it."

He takes a sip of his drink, and shakes his head as he swallows. "Don't believe everything you read, or see on television."

As soon as he says it, he swallows hard and says, "I'm sorry. I didn't mean anything by that."

I force a smile. "I know you didn't. It's okay. Most adults can read."

Reaching out, he takes my hand in his. "We're going to fix that."

I'm just hoping I'll be able to learn to read before our children do, because it would be humiliating to have to explain to our kids' teachers that their mother can't read. Luca has this idea that he can undo everything that was done to me, but he's wrong. He can't. As they say, you can't unring a bell. I'm willing to try for him, because I'm falling madly in love with this man. I have every reason to hate him, yet I don't. He is my happy place.

169

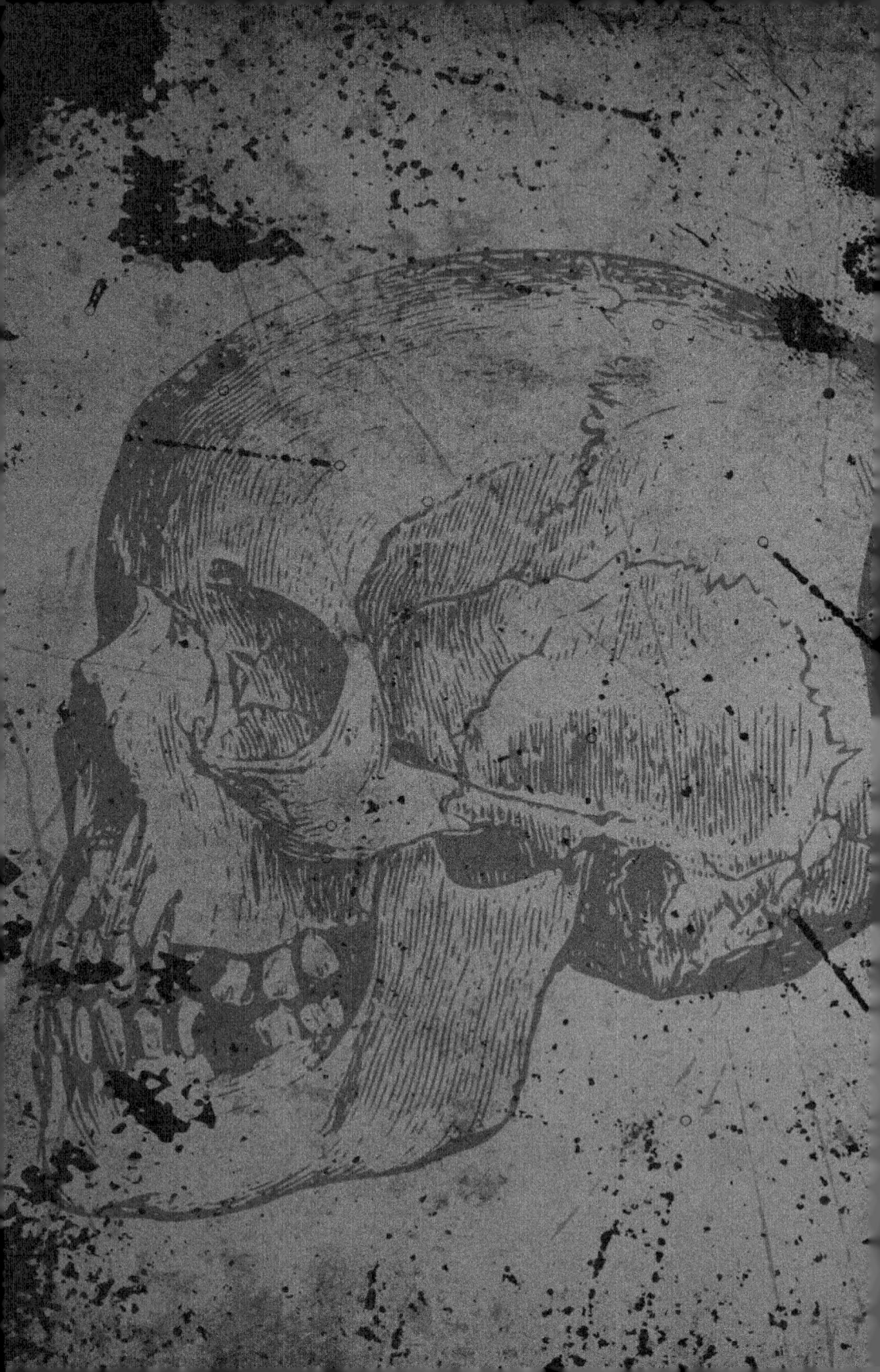

Chapter Thirty-One
BONES

Our server Miguel brings our food and sets it on the table in front of us. I chuckle as Athena's eyes get wide, as she stares at her plate in disbelief.

"This is too much, Luca. I can't eat this much."

I don't understand the issue with the amount of food on her plate.

"Eat what you can and leave the rest."

She gazes at me from across the table. "This is a waste, Luca. People are starving, and I'm going to throw half my food away. It's irresponsible."

Her expression is serious, so I don't laugh. "Would you like to donate money to the hungry?"

"Oh my god, could we?" she asks excitedly, and I nod because, fuck, if it makes her smile like that, I'll donate to any cause. Her face lights up and it makes my chest squeeze. Her right eye is black and blue, but the other smiles right along with her mouth. The right cheekbone below her eye is yellow and purple, but she's still gorgeous to me. My entire staff have been instructed to not stare and make my wife feel uncomfortable.

Athena takes a bite of pancake and chews with her eyes closed. I know this is likely making her think of her mother, so I ask her questions while she eats.

"Do you have any idea why she left?"

Her eyes pop open as she shakes her head. She swallows her food and says, "No idea."

"Was your father abusive to her?"

She laughs bitterly. "I don't know. I never saw him do anything to her, but of course he must have been. Knowing the things he did to me, I'm not sure he was ever capable of not being abusive."

I may regret my next question, but I need to know. "You told me Manny was your first. But your father?"

She shakes her head. "Really, Luca? Did you expect I would tell you my father took my virginity? Manny was my first in my mind, because back then he was sweet to me. I willingly gave him what he wanted. That was never the case with my father."

"One last question and then I'll stop."

She stares at me while she continues to eat, clearly more hungry than she realized.

"Did you never tell anyone about the abuse?"

I know she may not have had the opportunity if he wasn't even sending her to school, but if I find out anybody knew and did nothing, I'll kill them.

"William," she says with a heavy sigh, "I told him and he was disgusted with me. Like I had a choice. I honestly thought he'd try to help. Instead, he made me feel worse than I already did, and then fucked my mouth and called me a whore."

"William who?"

She shrugs. "Rothschild. I thought we meant something to each other, but it was one-sided."

Setting her fork down, she gazes at me with sad eyes. "I'm trash, Luca. I've always been used and abused like I don't matter. Even you knew that. It's probably what interested you. Let's not pretend that I matter to you all of a sudden, because you found me in a cage, getting the treatment you would have given me. Why did you think I didn't fight you the day you made me kneel in Manny's blood to suck your dick? It wasn't new. Give me your worst, and it's probably been done before. We can drop the charade. We both know what this is."

Her words make me feel two feet tall. I don't bother correcting her because she's not wrong. I never hit her and never would. Other than that, I've done the same things to her. I'd like to convince

172

myself that it's okay, because she's not my damn child. But deep down, I know it's not.

"Do you want to go into the pool?"

Her lips instantly lift into a smile. "Could we?"

I nod. "Whatever you want, baby. Your therapist will be here in a few hours. And my mother and sister would really like to see you later, but that's up to you."

"Can I wait until after therapy to decide?"

"Of course. Go into the tiki hut. There's a change room in there with a selection of bathing suits for you."

With the excitement of a kid on Christmas morning, she jumps up and heads into the hut to get changed. I am ready to go in the pool, since I was already wearing black swim shorts. I wait until my stunning wife walks toward me in a baby blue two-piece that makes my mouth water.

"Fucking gorgeous, Butterfly."

She flashes me a shy smile. "Thank you, Luca."

I grab her hand and pull her over to the pool. Taking the steps, we move into the heated water together. Wrapping my arms around her, just above her ass, I pull her in close to me. Leaning down, I kiss her neck before speaking directly into her ear, "I know you think I saw a victim and the predator that I am figured you were easy prey. That's not the case, baby. I know it might feel like you have 'victim' stamped on your forehead, but that's not what I saw. When I looked at you the very first time, I knew I was looking at pure beauty. That's what drew me in. It was all you. If I could go back and do things differently, I would. I can't rewrite history, but I can give you a future you deserve. You want to learn to read? Fine. You want to go to college? Fine. You want to go to the damn moon? I'll buy a fucking space shuttle and take you there myself."

She giggles in my arms. It's the kind of laugh that's with her whole body, and I love the way it feels as her body vibrates against mine.

"I don't think you can just buy a space shuttle, Luca."

I arch an eyebrow at her. "No? Maybe I'll have to steal one then."

Her laughter intensifies, making me feel like the luckiest asshole in the world. "I'm pretty sure you'd get caught really fast. And I'm equally positive you'd get us killed, because you do not know how to operate a space shuttle."

"Don't underestimate me, Butterfly. I will find a way to give you not only the moon, but every fucking star in the sky."

Athena gazes at me while running her fingers into the back of my hair. "I don't need the stars, Luca. I need this. You make me feel normal and safe. That's everything I need."

Sliding my hand into her hair, I'm careful to not hurt her, as I lean in and kiss her. With the slight hint of syrup, she tastes even sweeter than usual. She slides her tongue against mine while she moans and tugs on strands of my hair.

"Touch me, Luca," she asks, with closed eyes, after I pull away from our kiss.

I run my fingers down her arm, which only earns me a glare. "Touch me like you want me."

"Butterfly, it's too soon."

She laughs, but there's no joy behind it, only bitterness.

"You only like it if I don't want it? Is that it, Luca? Only when I beg you to stop do you want to fuck me? Either touch me like you fucking want me, or let me go."

I remove my hand from her arm and step back. A tear rolls down her cheek, and she turns away from me and leaves the pool. Standing like an idiot, I watch her walk away and go back inside the house.

I have a feeling that my wife thinks I don't want to touch her. I do. Fuck, I do. I'm not a therapist, so I don't know if this is normal behavior. I have no clue if she should be wanting me to touch her, and I have no idea how long I'm supposed to wait.

Stepping out of the pool, I feel like a goddamn failure. This was meant to be a perfect morning for Athena. Instead, I fucked it all up.

I drag a hand down my face as I walk back into the house, not even concerning myself with my wet body.

When I finally find Athena, she's curled up in a ball on the bed, crying.

"Butterfly."

She sits up, wrapping her arms around her legs, her gaze on her knees like she doesn't know I am here, but I know better than that.

The bed dips slightly from my weight as I sit beside her. "You need to give yourself time to work through this. Trust me, if I thought fucking you would make everything better, I'd already be inside you."

Athena blows out an exasperated breath. "I don't want you to be careful with me. Can't you just treat me like you used to?"

I arch an eyebrow at her, and she glares at me. "Not like that, asshole. Without chaining me to a wall or putting me in a cage."

Wrapping my hand around her throat, I narrow my gaze at her. "Let me be crystal fucking clear, Butterfly. I told you more than once not to call me that. I'm trying to be a good husband, but I won't tolerate my wife being a brat, and resorting to name calling."

She swallows hard against my hand and whispers, "I'm sorry."

"Good girl. Now, go take a shower. The therapist will be here soon."

Climbing off the bed, she walks toward the bathroom, but then stops and turns to me. "I'm sorry I ruined it, but thank you for letting me spend time outside."

With a nod, I say, "You're welcome. If you can control your tongue, we'll have dinner out there."

If she wants an asshole, I'm more than capable of that. The problem is, I don't think my wife knows what she wants. I know she wants to be treated normally, and I understand that, but I'm not sure she's ready to be. I'm concerned if I push her too far too fast, I'll lose her altogether. Not that I think she'll leave, because I don't.

However, I know if someone retreats inside themselves, they can go so far no one can reach them.

I need to talk to Penelope about this, which is the last fucking thing I want to do. She may be a psychologist, but she hates what I did to Athena. It's entirely possible that she'll tell me to go fuck myself.

Chapter Thirty-Two

ATHENA

Therapy isn't supposed to be fun, but for me it was really challenging. I didn't know how much to tell her about Luca, so I mostly didn't. I did ask her when we could have sex. The answer was generic; when I feel like I'm ready, and that he shouldn't push me for anything. It's not that I'm dying to have sex, it's just the normalcy of it. I don't want my husband to be afraid to touch me, or worse, think of my father when he does. Also, I think the longer we wait, the more likely it is to cause problems. Luca was the first man to look at me with unquenchable desire. The first to give me an orgasm. He was my first everything that counts, and I don't want to lose that.

I walk through the house looking for him, but I don't know where he is. Did he leave? I walk down the long upstairs hallway, peeking into each room as I pass, and stop in my tracks when I hear his angry, booming voice.

"I don't give a fuck. He was a goddamn pedophile, and raped his own fucking daughter. How many times? I have no clue, because she won't talk to me. If he has a problem with that asshole being dead, he can take it up with me, but no, he is not seeing my wife. Access fucking denied."

Standing outside the door, I shake as I attempt to figure out what he was talking about. Obviously, it was about me. But who wants to see me? I had no family aside from my mother and father. But he said, 'he is not seeing my wife'. I'm sure it was 'he' and not 'she'. Besides, why would my mother want anything to do with me now?

The door jerks open, and I come face to face with a furious Luca. His face is red, fists clenched, and I can feel the pure anger coming from him in waves. When he registers who is standing in front of him, he calms slightly. "Butterfly. Are you okay?"

I nod. "I'm fine. Are you okay?"

He grabs the back of my neck, pulls me close to him, and growls, "I am now."

Pressing his lips to mine, he kisses me aggressively, pushing his tongue into my mouth like he's ravenous for me. He cups my breast and pinches my nipple, causing me to whimper. Turning us around, he walks me backward until he pushes me down onto the top of a desk. Lifting my skirt, he slips his hand inside my panties and immediately finds my clit. I'm so turned on, I know it won't take long for me to explode. And then he stops. I glance at my surroundings, an 'L' shaped dark desk, a computer on the other side. A knife near my head?

"Fuck. I'm sorry," Luca says as he removes his hand from my panties.

He hovers over me, a hand on either side of the desk, appearing conflicted. Only moments ago, it was like an animal had taken over, and he couldn't control himself. I want the animal. I want him as desperate for me as I am for him. Reaching up beside my head, I grab the knife and press it to his chest, just holding it there, not attempting to cut him, and he stares at me, not with fear, but heat.

"Is that how we're playing this, wife?"

I don't respond with words, I simply watch him as he wraps his hand around mine. "Do it. Never threaten something you have no intention of following through on."

I nick his skin, and a few drops of blood come out, and my eyes grow wide with fear because I don't know how Luca will react. He runs his tongue over his lower lip, and stares at me with an intense gaze. "Do you remember how I told you pain turns me on, Butterfly?"

I nod slightly as I stare at the trickling blood blooming from his chest. It's beautiful, the dark ink with red blood breaking through. It's nearly hypnotizing.

"Give me the knife."

Without thinking about it, I do as he says, never considering what he's going to do next. I gasp as he takes the blade and cuts down the center of my dress with ease, before doing the same with my panties.

He holds the knife to my exposed breasts as I breathe heavily.

"I'm sorry."

The panic causes my body to tremble, as I wonder if he's going to kill me. If you had asked me even an hour ago if he'd ever hurt me, I would've said no, but now I'm not so sure.

Luca chuckles softly. "Rule number one is never threaten something you won't follow through on. Rule number two, beautiful Butterfly, is turnabout is fair play."

He pushes the knife into my skin, causing blood to bubble up, and I gasp from the burning sting. Leaning his head down, he licks at the blood with a groan. "Your blood is inside my body now. Mine will be in yours."

He moves so that his chest is over my mouth and, without him instructing me, I dart my tongue out and lick at the blood on his skin. The coppery taste should probably disgust me but it has the opposite effect.

Standing up, he removes his shorts, and I watch as his big cock springs free. He moves closer again, and surprises me when he makes a cut over my other breast, runs his finger through the small amount of blood, and smears it over my nipples.

He sucks one nipple into his mouth, and then the other, causing me to writhe beneath him.

"Luca," I moan. I need him inside me. It's like he lit a fire that won't go out until I have him completely.

"My wife is such a needy slut," he says with a smirk.

"Luca, please."

He tosses the knife onto the desk beside me, and grabs his cock and strokes it gently. "Is this what you want, Butterfly? You want me to fuck you until you can't remember your name?"

"Yes," I moan, "I need you. Please, Luca."

I spread my legs wide and he lines his cock up with my entrance, then he pushes inside me, and we both groan together like it's the first time, as he bottoms out. Luca grips underneath my thighs and pushes my legs back, pinning them so I can't move, and pulls out and slams back inside me.

"Fuck. This pussy is like a goddamn drug."

Wrapping his hand around my throat, he stares into my eyes as he continues his hard thrusts. "You've ruined me, Butterfly. The man I was is gone. You made me fall so fucking in love with you, I can't see anything else. If I could devour you, so I could always have you with me, I would. If I could live inside you, I would. I've never believed in anything. With you, I somehow know, I loved you in another lifetime. I didn't know it at the time, but I was searching for you; the piece I didn't even know was missing."

Grabbing the back of his head, I pull him down to me. "I love you."

He presses his lips to mine in a kiss that sets my soul on fire. His tongue slides against mine, as he moves inside me with the occasional groan of pleasure.

Breaking our kiss, he watches me with a dark unreadable expression. "Mine. My wife. Forever."

I run my fingers through his hair, which I know he loves, and he growls in my ear, "Fucking come for me. Give me everything you have."

"Luca," I cry out, as he rails into me hard and fast. He bites my neck and I come undone beneath him. His chest covering mine, his weight on top of me, the heavy breaths in my ear, every bit of him is everything I need. Gripping my face hard, he holds me so I can't move.

"I can't get enough of you. Why can't I get enough? This is the closest I can get, and it makes me insane. The more I have you, the more I fucking need you."

A tear rolls down my cheek and he doesn't miss a beat. He quickly darts his tongue out and licks up my cheek.

"I love your tears, wife, but why are you crying?"

I giggle softly. "Relief, mostly. I thought I had lost this. That you'd never want me again."

He shakes his head in disbelief. "Silly Butterfly. I will always want you. Every time I come inside your beautiful cunt, I'm only thinking about doing it again."

I wrap my arms around his neck, holding him close to me, as his body shakes with slight tremors and he spasms inside me.

Luca places his hand on the side of my face, and stares at me affectionately. "Please tell me you're okay. I don't want to hurt you. All I want to do is take every ounce of pain from you."

"I'm okay. I promise. I wasn't broken the day we met, and I'm not broken now. The only thing I can't handle is the cage and restraints. Cut me. Make me bleed. I've lived through far worse."

Pulling out of me, he stands and lifts me into his arms. "Where are we going?" I ask.

He chuckles softly. "To get you dressed before my mother and sister stop by. I told them to wait for an invitation, but they are insistent on making sure you are okay."

I gasp as he carries me out of the room. "Oh my god, do they know everything?"

"No, baby," he says as he climbs the stairs, "Not entirely. They know the state we found you in, so it's probably not hard to guess, but I certainly have not told them everything. I have a feeling I don't even know everything. I hope one day you'll trust me enough to tell me."

I place my arms around his neck and press my face into his chest. "I don't know if you need those mental images."

Stopping momentarily, he stares at me. "And I don't think you need to keep it locked within yourself. You can let me in, so I can help carry the burden."

"I'll try. After your family leaves."

He kisses me on the forehead. "Thank you."

With a smirk, he says, "We'll shower and then bandage up your beautiful breasts, because it would appear someone cut them."

Giggling, I say, "He was an animal."

Setting me down, he chuckles. "And he will be again."

Luca reaches into the shower and turns the water on. Once he's satisfied it's the right temperature, he tells me, "Ladies first."

I step under the hot water and he gets in behind me, dragging his fingers down my back to my ass, as he towers over me and speaks in a husky voice, directly in my ear.

"Has anybody been inside this beautiful ass?"

I shake my head, splashing water from my hair. "No."

Glancing over my shoulder, I watch as he kneels behind me and spreads my cheeks. "What are you-"

My sentence ends with a moan, as he flicks his tongue over my back hole.

"Luca."

"And you're going to let your husband take it, aren't you, Butterfly?"

"Yes," I cry out as he pushes his tongue inside me.

Reaching around, he rubs my clit while moving his tongue in circles inside my ass. This shouldn't feel so good, but it does. Placing my hands on the wall for support, I'm consumed by my orgasm. By him. It's at this moment that I realize what he said to me before was right. My life has changed in every way. And it's all because of my husband. If he wants children, I'll give them to him willingly, because there is nothing I wouldn't do for him.

Chapter Thirty-Three

BONES

I rise to my full height, and wrap my arm around her waist, while kissing her neck and enjoying every moan.

"If I had time, I'd fuck you again. Fucking families."

Athena leans her head back over my shoulder with a sweet giggle. "It's sweet though that they care enough to check on me."

Shaking my head, I tell her the truth, "It's sweet now, until they smother you with love and affection. It will get old."

She turns in my arms and gazes at me with a longing expression. "No, Luca, it won't. I haven't had anyone that cared about whether I lived or died since I was a little girl. Maybe not even then, but at least when I was little, they pretended. It will never get old because no matter how much time passes, I will learn to live with what happened, but I'll never forget. Maybe one day, the memory of the torture will fade, along with the bruises, but I don't think not mattering to anyone ever will."

Her words take the breath from my lungs. I take her in my arms and hold her, because I don't know what else to do.

"I'm sorry. This never should have happened to you. It shouldn't happen to anyone, but it really shouldn't have happened to you. You're so good and perfect. I'm sorry."

Tilting her head back, she gazes at me with her hands on my chest. "You make it better, Luca. I'm okay. Please don't worry about me."

I kiss her softly. "Good. Maybe you can convince the women in my family that I haven't hurt you. So they don't take my balls."

Athena giggles sweetly, making my chest constrict. "Don't worry, big bad Bones, I'll protect you."

I cup her cheeks. "If any other woman said that I'd laugh, but you are the strongest woman I've ever met. And I believe you would if you thought it was necessary."

I grab the body wash and cleanse every inch of her body, trying to ignore her little moans, because my family will be here soon. She does the same for me, stopping to stroke my cock, causing me to bite the inside of my cheek.

"Rinse off, get dry, and dress, because if I stare at your naked body much longer, I'll be inside you again."

She gets out, and I rinse myself before turning the water off, and getting out. She puts two bandaids on her pretty tits, and I growl, "Next time, I do that."

Athena turns to me with surprise. "Why?"

I scowl at her. "If I hurt you, I'll be the one to make it better."

"It's barely a cut. I probably don't even need to cover them."

While drying my body with the fluffy white towel, I say, "Can you do as you're told?"

"Fine," she sighs as she exits the bathroom.

I shake my head as I watch her disappear. *Beautiful fucking brat. And all mine.*

I'm not honestly worried about my mother or my sister trying to hurt me, but one thing does scare me. If they try to do the right thing and take her from me, I don't know how I'd react. I'd never hurt them, but I can't let her leave either.

I walk into the bedroom and find Athena sitting on the bed, dressed in a light blue dress with flowers scattered on the print. Grabbing boxers, I pull them on. "Are you okay, baby?"

She sighs audibly as I finish getting dressed.

"Athena?"

"Yeah, I'm okay. It's just, I never really talked to them before, and what if they don't like me?"

I can't help but chuckle. "That's what you're worried about? They will love you. Chances are very good they'll prefer you over me."

184

Grabbing my phone, I check the notifications and realize that they're here.

"Trust me. Everything will be fine, but it's time to go downstairs, because my mom and sister are here."

ATHENA

We walk downstairs, and I stand back as Luca opens the door to let his mother and sister inside. He kisses both of them on the cheek, and his mother glares at him. "Always happy to see my son, but I'm here for my daughter."

"Of course you are," he says, feigning annoyance.

She rushes over to me and grabs me in a tight hug. "You poor thing. Are you okay?"

I nod as she pulls away, and Penelope hugs me, before glaring at her brother. "Is he treating you okay?"

Luca shakes his head as he walks back to the massive living room area. "Come sit down. You can continue your interrogation in comfort."

The three of us follow him, and he motions for me to sit beside him. His mother and sister sit on the other end watching us.

Penelope stares at the marks on my face, and I worry she thinks my husband did this to me.

"He didn't cause these bruises."

She smiles softly. "I know that. I'm well aware of what my brother is capable of, and beating a woman isn't in his bag of tricks."

Luca puts his arm around me and holds me close to him. "The problem has been taken care of."

His sister looks at me with concern. "Do you have someone to talk to?"

I smile softly as Luca squeezes my shoulder affectionately. "Luca hired a therapist for me. I saw her earlier today."

Her face registers surprise, but she smiles. "Good."

Luca's mother looks at him with obvious disappointment. "I know everything, Luca. You have always known I wanted you to marry for love, not for money, or to become the head of the family. Marriage should never be a business arrangement. You made this woman, who has already been through hell, marry you. I can only imagine how you achieved this."

Leaning down, he kisses my cheek. "I love my wife very much. We did not marry for love, but I love her now. Does anything else really matter?"

Her gaze turns to me. "Are you here against your will, Athena?"

My eyes widen at her direct question, and I shake my head.

"No. I love Luca. There is nowhere else I want to be."

It's the truth. Of course, it didn't start out that way, and I will never tell his mother the things he did to me in the beginning, because while they seem to think they know what he's capable of, I doubt they really do. Not to that extent anyway.

His mother releases a relieved sigh. "Very well. Tell me about yourself. What do you like to do?"

I glance at Luca, because I'm unsure how to answer her. Clearly, I don't want her to know I've lived in captivity for so long, that I don't really know what I like to do. It should be an easy question, but it's not. Even when I was with Manny, I wasn't free.

My husband saves me and says, "She loves the outdoors. We spent the morning outside today."

"I enjoy shopping too, but I don't like spending enormous amounts of money like some people."

Luca chuckles as he pulls me even closer. "You'll get used to it, Butterfly."

Penelope says, "We should go shopping next weekend. Shopping and lunch. Just the two of us."

I glance at him, waiting for him to say no, but instead, he chuckles. "It won't be just the two of you. My wife goes nowhere without security."

She waves her hand in the air. "That's fine. And probably wise."

We sit comfortably, talking about everything from the day his father bought this house for Luca, to what he was like as a boy, and his lack of dating experience. I'm tempted to ask how his father is doing, but I don't, because I don't want to upset anyone. I'm sure it's difficult for all of them to know he's going to die. While I don't have experience with a close family, I can tell they are one.

When they stand to leave, both Luca and I join them. His mother smiles at me fondly. "Welcome to the family, *figlia*."

Luca glances at me and mouths, 'daughter'.

"Thank you."

She hugs me and whispers in my ear, "I'm sorry you had the family you did. We are your family now. You're my daughter. If you need anything, you call me."

I'm overcome with emotion when they leave. My heart is full after hearing her say that to me. For a moment, I allow myself to feel like I matter. I've always thought your family is the one you were born into. Maybe it doesn't have to be though. For the first time, in possibly my entire life, I have hope for the future. It's a foreign feeling, but one I welcome.

Once he says goodbye to his family, he turns to me with a grin. "Dinner outside as promised?"

"I was wondering if we could go out for dinner."

He wraps his arms around my waist and pulls me in, until my body is pressed against his. "Whatever you want, baby."

I sigh as I return his embrace. "I was hoping you might help me read the menu. I don't want Penelope to know. And if she wants to go for lunch, I'll need to read the menu."

"Of course," he says, as he leans down and kisses my neck.

"She will likely want to go to Manhattan's, so I'll take you there."

Chapter Thirty-Four

BONES

Athena sits beside me at Manhattan's, which is a seafood restaurant that my sister is obsessed with. Our table is right beside a massive saltwater fish tank my wife seems quite drawn to. The restaurant isn't a fancy one like she probably expected, but it's still nice. The ceiling has murals painted of the ocean, and the many creatures you find there. It's like *Finding Nemo* in real life. The tables are all square, dark wood, and covered with white tablecloths. We sit with wine and menus in front of us, but Athena clearly is in no hurry.

I place my arm around her and speak low into her ear, so nobody overhears me. If I can avoid her embarrassment, I will.

"You don't need to worry about Penelope judging you because you can't read. It's not your fault, and my sister isn't a bitch. If anything, she'd want to help you."

Athena turns her head to me. "I know, but I don't want anyone to know, Luca. It kills me that you know."

I kiss her briefly on the lips. "Whatever you want. I'm going to find you a tutor tomorrow. I know this bothers you, and we're going to rectify this."

She smiles at me and surprises me. "I wish we had a pen and paper. I want to see the word butterfly."

Holding up my hand, I motion for the waitress, and she comes over.

"Do you have a pen and paper we can use?"

She pulls a pen and paper from her black apron, and sets it on the table before she walks away. I'm not sure if she was inconvenienced but I don't care.

I spell out the word she wants to see, and just below it, I separate the word for her; writing 'but-ter-fly'. Of course, I have no idea how to teach someone how to read, but I remember as a kid having to sound things out.

She sits staring at the paper in awe, like the word is magical. It was never meant to be a nickname that stuck. Hell, I never planned to keep her. Now I know she'll always be my Butterfly, but instead of destroying her, I'll protect her. With my life, if necessary. Everyone who hurt my wife will die, her mother included. No one is safe. If I find out a million more people hurt her, then I'll kill a million people. There's no limit. Nothing will ever be too much.

I sound out the word, and point to the different letters as I sound it out, and she smiles softly. "I think that's my favorite word."

Stroking my fingers down her cheek, I ask, "Are you sure it isn't words like pussy? Or fuck? Harder?"

Her cheeks turn bright red, as she glances around to see if anyone heard me, and then she glares at me. "Luca!"

I chuckle as I kiss her forehead. "And that's my favorite word."

"Teach me the food words before she comes back."

I open the menu and point out the different sections. "These are appetizers. Soups, salads, breads, and things like that."

Continuing to point, I say, "These are the entrees. The main item of your meal. Penelope's favorite is the baked salmon. Lobster. Crab Legs. Fish of the Day. Today is Thursday, so it's Trout. It shows underneath. When you come with my sister, it'll probably be Sunday, so it's going to be Pan Roasted Haddock."

She blinks away unshed tears as she whispers. "This is impossible, Luca. I can't do this."

I take her chin in my hand and tilt her head back gently. "You can and you will. Let's go through it again."

I spend an hour helping her try to read the words, but I know it's more about her memorizing it, than learning it. She'll need to be taught the basics of reading by a professional. Hopefully, I've helped

190

enough so she can enjoy her day with my sister, rather than feeling bad about herself. I don't love that she's going to be out of the house for an entire day without me, but I have to let her live a life. She has been kept as a prisoner for long enough. I'm hoping that, as she gets to know my sister better, that she'll open up to her and tell her the truth. It will be good for Athena to have a woman around that she can talk to.

After we order, she visibly relaxes beside me.

She giggles. "I hope I like lobster, because I'll probably order that when I come again because it'll be easier."

"You've never had it then?"

She rolls her eyes at me. "No, Luca. Of course I haven't."

With anyone else, I'd give them a lecture about eating the bottom feeders of the ocean. They are disgusting. They'll eat each other, for fuck's sake. The time will likely come when I do tell her that, but not right now. I don't want to make things more difficult for her.

After she finishes half a glass of wine, I decide it's time to dig for information.

"How did you meet William?"

She takes another gulp of wine before she answers, "My father was friends with his mother, and she wanted a friend for her son. He had trouble socializing. Those were my first outings."

"How old were you?"

Her eyes dart up to the ceiling as if she'll find the answer there, and then she shrugs. "I'm not sure, but I think fourteen or fifteen."

"And you told him?"

She nods slightly. "We had gotten close, or I thought we had. I really thought he'd help me. Maybe call the police or something."

"I'm going to find him."

Athena's eyes widen with apparent shock. "You don't have to. It's in the past."

I chuckle as I run my fingers down her bare arm. "That's not how it works, Butterfly. They hurt you, they die. It's simple. No one is safe."

She looks at me like I'm insane, and bites, "So if someone cuts in front of me in line, you'll kill them?"

I shrug while I smirk at her. "It's a possibility."

I'm not as much of an animal as my wife seems to think I am. I wouldn't really kill someone for cutting in line, although I might threaten it. I'm not kidding though, if someone hurts her, they'll pay the price. And William is next on my list. Then her mother.

She takes my hand. "I need you to promise me something."

I'm an idiot, so I nod in agreement, without asking what she wants. "Anything."

The fact is, there's very little I wouldn't give my wife. Her happiness means everything to me, so I didn't hesitate even though I should have.

"Leave my mother alone, Luca. I don't want you to hurt her."

I swallow hard. "Butterfly, I can't promise that."

"You already did."

"Athena," I growl, "She left you there. She could have taken you with her, and would have spared you everything you've been through."

Reaching up, she runs her delicate fingers through my hair. She knows this is a weakness for me. Every time she does this, I nearly lose my mind.

"I love you, Luca. And I love that you want to protect me, that you want to somehow right the past, but I need you to not hurt her. Please."

Closing my eyes, I sigh audibly. "Fine."

"Thank you."

"Do you want a relationship with her? Is that why?"

I open my eyes and find her staring at me, but she looks so far away.

"No. I will never forgive her for abandoning me the way she did, but I don't want her to die. She had reasons for what she did, I'm sure of it. Whatever the case, I forgive her, but forgiving her doesn't mean having her in my life."

"For now, baby, I'll leave her alone, but if she ever tries to hurt you again, I may go back on my word."

She takes a sip of her wine, and sets the glass back on the table before returning her gaze to mine. "I can live with that. Now, who wanted to see me?"

I look away from her and try to pretend I didn't hear her, because this isn't a conversation I want to have with her, but she persists.

"Luca, when I was standing outside your office, I heard you. I don't know who you were talking about, but I know it involved me."

"I will tell you everything you need to know."

Athena folds her arms over her chest as she glares at me with obvious irritation. "If it's about me, I should know. Please don't keep secrets from me. That's not the kind of marriage I want."

I exhale a deep breath. "You have a brother that is snooping around and asking questions, because he's pissed his father is dead."

She gasps. "A brother? I don't have a brother, Luca."

"He had a child with another woman before your mother left. He's two years older than you are."

"What does he want from me?"

I hate the look of fear on her face, which is why I didn't want to tell her.

"It doesn't matter. Reaper is on him. He will take care of it. He will not live long enough to hurt you."

Instead of the response I expect, she gets up and climbs onto my lap, ignoring the people in the restaurant, and wraps her arms around my neck. "Thank you."

Winding her hair around my fist, I pull her closer and taste her lips. I lick them before pushing my tongue into her mouth. The waitress brings our food, but we don't stop, so she sets the colorful plates down and walks away. Athena runs her fingers into the back of my hair and I groan in frustration, because I'm tempted to fuck her right here. She pulls back with a giggle. "Sorry. I was feeling grateful."

I nod to her chair. "You better sit down and eat, before you're feeling something entirely different."

"Animal," she says quietly.

Chapter Thirty-Five

ATHENA

Five days later…

I'm just saying goodbye to my tutor, Ashley, when Luca walks in and the anger running through him is visible. After she leaves, I ask him, "What's wrong?"

"Do you think you can manage to go back to the basement?"

I back away slowly. "Luca, please."

"Jesus, Butterfly, no. I have someone down there to deal with. It's not like that."

I try to calm my racing heart, that feels like it's in my throat, as he approaches me and pulls me into his arms. "I'm sorry. I didn't mean to scare you. I promised you, never again. I never break my promises."

Hugging him back, I let him calm me. His touch, his scent. All of my husband soothes me like a magical ointment for my soul.

"It's William," he says.

I let go of him. "I can't. Don't make me face him."

He wraps his hand around my chin and tilts my head back. "Look at me, Butterfly."

I do and he says, "Don't you get it? You have nothing to fear. You are the most powerful mafia wife. We will go down there, and you will instruct me on how you want his pain delivered. He holds no power over you. You are about to become the queen of the Bonetti empire. Don't shy away from it, fucking own it. Everything you want is within your grasp. Take it."

I straighten my shoulders and try to do as he says, but I'm not an idiot, so I ask, "Is he restrained?"

He smirks at me. "As if I'd let him be in the same room with my wife if he weren't."

Luca takes my hand in his. "Come, Mrs. Bonetti. Let's go play my favorite game. Revenge."

We walk across the house, and as we get to the door to the basement, I take a deep breath.

"You good, wife?"

I nod with a smile. "I'm good, husband."

He starts whistling as we walk down the stairs and I giggle. "Why do you do that?"

With a chuckle, he admits, "It tends to freak them out. I may be an asshole after all, because I enjoy the fear."

When we reach the bottom and walk into the room, I immediately recognize him. He has the same dark hair, blue eyes, and muscular physique, just an older version of the boy I knew. His normal cocky expression is replaced with one of terror as he trembles in his chair. William's feet are chained to the same wall I once was, but he doesn't have much give. There's a table in front of him and his arms are each in a blue vise. I don't question what they will be used for, because I'm sure I'll figure it out soon enough.

"Thank you for waiting," Luca says, and I giggle, because it's not like he had a whole lot of choice in the matter.

"Please. Let me go."

My husband waves his hand to me. "Everything that happens today is my wife's choice. Whatever she tells me to do will be done. So I suggest you beg her instead of me."

He raises his head and looks at me through tear filled eyes. "Athena, please. I never hurt you, that was your dad."

Placing my hands on my hips, I glare at him. "You raped me."

He shakes his head fearfully, as he glances at Luca. "I never. Why would you say that? I never even fucked you."

Arching an eyebrow at him, I attempt to help him with his memory. "You fucked my mouth without consent. What would you call that?"

He looks at me with shock. It's clear that he really doesn't believe he did anything wrong.

"That's not even rape."

The fact that he is so clueless is disgusting, and just tells me Luca should not let him live. How many women has he done this to? I probably don't want to know.

Luca steps in front of him. "You could've helped her, but instead you made her feel disgusting for things she didn't choose. Knowing she was a victim, you chose to victimize her again."

I watch as he starts turning a knob and the plates move closer. There's a faint distant memory of my father using these, when he tinkered in his garage when I was tiny. As the plates touch both sides of his arms, I figure out what's happening, and it's going to hurt.

"Wait!" He screams.

"Just fucking wait."

His face is covered in snot and tears, as he scrambles for the right thing to say, but his words are the last thing I expect.

"You wouldn't do this to your brother. I'm your brother, Athena. We are family."

"What?" I ask, while the confusion clouds my brain. He's not related to me. Why is he saying that?

"I've been trying to figure out why my dad was killed. That's why I was brought here, right?"

"What?"

William screams louder this time, as if I couldn't hear him. "I'm your fucking brother. I was born first. Dad chose your mom over mine and look how that turned out. Now let me go."

I glance at my husband in disbelief, and he shrugs. "That's quite the plot twist, wife. Does it change anything for you?"

197

Shaking my head, I say, "It does not. Like father, like son, I suppose. Continue."

Luca turns the knob on his left arm as William screams. I smile at him because he deserves this. Even if he hadn't done what he did to me, I know Luca would never let him live because he's a threat to my safety, and one day when we have children, to their safety as well.

"Take a seat, Butterfly. This won't be quick."

I do as he says, and watch as he breaks William's arm. The first time I witnessed this, I was afraid, because I didn't know if I was next. I know better now. Occasionally, the fear tries to reappear, like when he mentioned the basement. It's like a programmed response, but in my heart, I know my husband will never hurt me.

He moves to the other arm, and begins the same process he just did with William's left arm. I listen as he screams for me to help. "Athena!"

I smile at him again. "I'm going to give you the same help you gave me when I asked for it. None."

Leaning forward with interest, I watch as the sound of bone crunching echoes in the room, and my brutal husband moves back to his left arm, releases the vise, pulls him down by his arm, and locks his bicep into the device. I watch a shirtless Luca begin tightening the vise again, and he is hot as hell. He moves with little effort, his jaw relaxed, and his eyes darting between William and me. He flashes me a delicious smirk. "Wanna help?"

I nod and he puts William's right bicep in the vise like he did the other, and motions for me to come over to him. Walking over to Luca, he guides me. "It's easy. You turn the knob over and over until you hear crushing. Once the plates hit his arm, it gets harder to turn. That takes strength, but I'll help you."

William's face is bright red and drenched with sweat. His head hangs down on the table, his expression one of complete defeat as he pants heavily. He knows it's over. The moment I agreed to help

Luca, he knew there was no way his life would be spared. Maybe I should feel bad but I don't. In fact, I bet he knew what was going on before I even told him. And yet he did nothing. Luca was right; as the plates begin to touch his arm, it gets hard to turn, so he takes over and places my hand over his, and seems to turn it without any trouble at all.

Our pathetic victim sobs against the table, but he doesn't bother begging for mercy anymore. He knows it's useless.

"Finish him," I say to Luca.

He pulls a knife from his back pocket. "You sure?"

I nod slightly. "Yes."

With a grin, he gazes at me. "Grab his hair and pull his head back for me."

I do as he says, and grab onto his hair as tight as I can and pull his head back, while Luca quickly slashes his throat and instructs me, "Let go."

His head smashes into the table with a loud thump, as the blood pools onto the table and pours onto the floor.

Luca stares at me with a heated expression, as he grabs his phone and makes a call, never taking his eyes from mine. "There's a body in the basement for you to take care of."

I flash him a questioning look, and he takes my hand in his and pulls me to the basement stairs. "I would do it myself, but I'm going to be very busy fucking my wife."

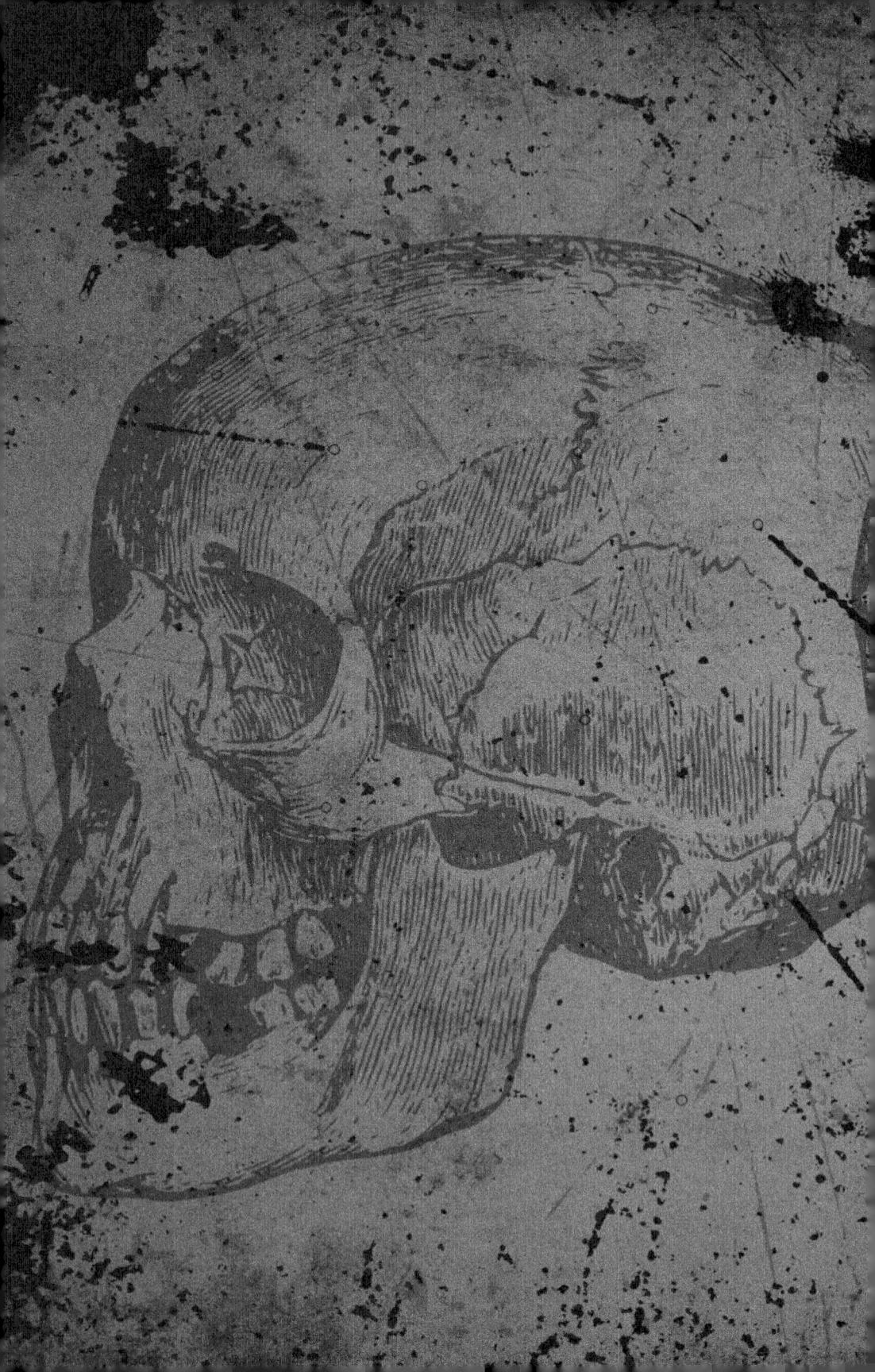

Chapter Thirty-Six
BONES

Three weeks later...

There is one section of the house I have kept from my wife intentionally. At first, it was an oversight, but the second I came up with this plan, I made sure to keep her away from it. I had to get her out of the house for a while today so I, along with Eduardo, could set it up without her asking questions. Now that everything is ready to go and I've told Penelope to bring her back, I'm riddled with nerves. Will she like this? Or will she think it's stupid? I have never second guessed myself more times than I have in the last six hours.

Athena and Penelope walk in the door, and the relief I feel is instant. I have no fucking idea how she does this to me. Charging straight for her, I scoop her into my arms and slam my lips to hers.

My sister laughs. "Jesus, Bones. She went shopping for six hours. It's not like she was away at war."

I ignore her, and kiss the hell out of my wife. When I pull away, her cheeks are flushed, as she looks at me with a dazed expression. "Wow. I should leave more often."

Penelope says, "I'm going to leave before I see things I will never unsee. Athena, I'll call you. Bones, behave."

I chuckle as she turns and heads out the door. Grabbing Athena's hand, I pull her across the house to the stairs.

She giggles softly. "What is up with you?"

"I want to show you something."

I take her to the farthest wing of the house and open the doors, and hear her gasp, "Oh my god, Luca."

ATHENA

We step out onto a balcony that extends from the outside of the house. It's massive, with a built-in railing that is made of the same stone as the pillars at the front of the house. There's a fire pit in the middle, burning firewood, probably because it's gotten colder over the last few weeks. There's a glass bar off to the right, with several bottles of alcohol on it. The floor is covered with a large blanket, and two glasses of wine on the floor beside it. Luca pulls me to the blanket, sits down and pulls me on top of him, before handing me a drink. I say thank you and put it down beside me.

He stares at me with confusion. "It's your favorite, Butterfly."

I move my legs around him so I'm straddling his lap, and stroking my fingers down his face. "Thank you. It was very thoughtful."

He continues staring at me, like he doesn't understand me at all, so I just blurt it out.

"Luca, I'm pregnant."

His breathing picks up as he nearly whispers, "Say that again."

"I'm pregnant. I can't drink wine, because it's not good for our baby."

"Goddamn it, Butterfly."

My heart falls, in fact, I'm not sure it's even beating at this moment.

I withdraw from him. "I thought this is what you wanted. You don't want our baby?"

"I knew I'd fuck everything up."

He takes a deep breath and waves his hand in the air. "I was supposed to give you everything. The moon, the stars in the sky, and instead, once again, you give me the entire fucking world."

Glancing up, I realize what he's talking about as I release a gasp. Right above us is the most perfect sky, sparkling with millions of stars and a full moon.

"Luca. This is beautiful."

He reaches out and touches my still flat stomach. "No. This is beautiful."

Standing up and taking me with him, he turns around and lays me on the blanket, and unzips the zipper on the side of my dress that starts from the top and goes to the bottom.

He spreads my legs, and kneels between them as he removes his shirt, while dragging his eyes down my body, before bringing them back up to my face.

"I will never understand how a woman that had everything taken from her has managed to give all of herself to a man like me. I don't deserve you. I never did. Maybe I never will, but I swear to you I'm going to do everything I can to make you happy."

Climbing over me, he gazes at me with obvious adoration, and I say, "You already do, Luca."

Pressing his hand to the side of my face, he groans, "You've given me a child. Made me a father. Whatever you need, tell me and it's yours. You want your feet rubbed? Done. Ice cream at two in the morning? Whatever it is, I'll do it."

"I need my husband inside me."

He removes himself from his pants, slides my panties to the side, and lines his cock up with my entrance.

"I'll make the sacrifice," he says with a chuckle, before he slides into me. Hovering over me with a hand on either side of me, he fucks me slowly. It's quiet outside, with only the sounds of our heavy breathing, and the crackling fire.

"Luca," I moan, as I run my fingers into the back of his hair, "I love you."

He picks up his speed, and with every thrust, he hits my clit, causing me to moan.

"I love you too, Butterfly. I think I have since I saw you hanging upside down on my wall."

My pussy clenches down on his cock as my orgasm builds, and he grunts his release while he stares at me.

"I was wrong. Butterflies aren't too fragile for life. You will survive the monsters of our world, because I'll protect you until my last breath. No one will ever hurt you again, because you're mine."

He rolls over to his back and pulls me with him, and wraps his arms around me. I sigh contentedly, because this is far more than I ever imagined my life could turn out to be. I lived a life of abuse, only ever hoping to survive another day. Happiness was never in my wildest dreams, because it seemed too far out of reach.

When Luca first mentioned having children, I was scared. How could I know I would never abandon my children like my mother did with me? When I looked down at the pregnancy test, with Penelope hovering over me, I knew the answer. One little word, *pregnant*, and I knew I already loved this baby. I will probably never know why she did what she did. And that's okay, because my happiness doesn't come from the people that gave me life. It's in the family I'm creating with Luca.

"Marry me again."

"What?" I say, popping my head up to look into his face.

"Marry me again, because you love me and want to spend the rest of your life with me. Not because you have threats hanging over your head. We can do it anywhere you want."

I can't help the grin that overtakes my face. "I'll marry you again, Luca."

The End

Epilogue One
BONES

When we planned our wedding for the first day of December, I had no idea my father would die only days before, on Thanksgiving day. Athena was insistent we postpone our ceremony, but my mother wouldn't have it.

"Figlio, no. At a time like this, we need to surround ourselves with love. What's a better demonstration of love than a wedding? Besides, your father would be angry if you cancel it, because he will be there. He'll be looking down on you with pride."

I told Athena we could do our second wedding anywhere in the world. It was about what she wanted. I would've taken her to Italy, Greece, France, literally anywhere you can get to by plane, but she wanted to do it here at our home, on the balcony she fell in love with only a few short months ago.

I stand in front of the railing, waiting for my bride. I'm not nervous about marrying her because obviously I've already done that. What worries me the most, and has my anxiety at its peak, is my concern that Athena is happy. The need for today to be everything she wants it to be is intense. There aren't a lot of people here, because Athena wanted to keep it small. We have white wooden chairs set up between an aisle with a red carpet. Every queen should have a red carpet to walk down. The De Luca brothers and their wives sit on one side. My buddies Sin and Zade sit on the other side with their wives. I don't have to worry about Athena being alone today, because my mother and sister are with her. They wouldn't have it any other way. Two of my three brothers stand beside me, but I'm beginning to wonder where the other one is. I ask, Psycho, "Where the fuck is Reaper?"

He shrugs. "No idea. He'll be here."

Finally, my missing brother comes running in, and I question him, "Where the fuck were you?"

With a grin, he says, "Saying hello to my sister-in-law. I've never told you, but she has beautiful eyes."

I turn to him with a glare. "Fucking freak. Don't look at my wife's eyes. I'll cut your fucking dick off and shove it down your throat."

He chuckles loudly. "Calm your tits. I'm not going to hurt my little sister. Besides, it's not *her* eyes I want."

Right. Living dead girl.

Shaking my head, I turn away from him and mutter under my breath. "You're not alright, man."

All thoughts of my brother disappear when I spot my sister coming in to sit down. I watch the doorway like a hawk, and finally my bride enters with my mother beside her. My heart squeezes as I watch my wife and mother smiling at each other fondly. Everything Athena's mother never was for her, my mother is now. If anyone in the outside world saw them together, they would be sure she and Athena were biological mother and daughter. Not because they look alike, but because the bond between them is that strong. It's the same with her and my sister.

Athena looks over to where I stand with my brothers. Her eyes find mine, and she smiles warmly, as her cheeks fill with a beautiful rosy color. I don't know if it's from an emotion, or because it's cold, since it's December. The firepit is going, but the air is still chilled. She wanted to do this at night, so we could say our vows underneath the stars.

Of course, my wife always looks stunning and today is no different. She stands at the entrance, waiting for the music to start, wearing a white lace gown with a sexy 'v' neck. It's strapless, but she has a fur shawl over her shoulders to keep her warm. While I hadn't seen the dress, when she told me it had no sleeves, I demanded she find a new dress because I don't want her to be cold, and get sick. I've been told I'm over the top more than once, but I don't care. When it comes to protecting her from everything, even the cold air, I take it seriously. And it's not just about her anymore. She is carrying our daughter. If she thinks I'm over the top with her, she hasn't seen anything yet.

The piano starts playing the music she selected, and she begins to walk down the aisle with my mother by her side, which is a good thing, because I was coming close to charging toward her and taking her in my arms, long before our priest says I can.

They stop at the end of the aisle, and my mother kisses her on the cheek before she takes a seat in the front row. I watch my mom pick up the picture of my father sitting on the chair beside her. She stares at it affectionately before wiping a tear away. She catches my gaze and nods, letting me know she's okay, which I doubt, because I know losing my father broke her heart. She dedicated her entire life to him, and loved him fiercely. We will all make sure she's okay. Currently, she is staying a week at each of our houses, and soon she'll decide where she'll live permanently. At first she fought us on it because she can take care of herself, but the fact is she's getting old, and none of us think her living in a big house by herself is good for her.

I take Athena's hand and lean down to whisper in her ear, because my words are for her and her alone.

"You look beautiful, Butterfly. I can't wait to get rid of all these people, and tear this dress off your stunning body."

Her cheeks heat as she lowers her head in embarrassment. "Luca," she scolds me, and I love it. Nothing I say should surprise her at this point, but I like that I can still get this reaction out of her.

We both chose to say a few things to each other before the priest conducts his ceremony, and he tells her she can go first.

She stares into my eyes as she speaks quietly, but from her heart.

"My life before you was a living hell. I never dared to dream of the life I have now, because you should only dream things that are attainable. This is beyond anything I could have imagined. It's all because you saved me. I would have died there. You took an illiterate, broken butterfly and healed her. You showed me what love is, and gave me a beautiful family. For that, I will be eternally grateful. Thank you for loving me the way you do. Please, don't ever stop."

I swallow hard, and barely hear the priest tell me it's my turn.

"I couldn't stop if I tried, Butterfly. I told you before I thought I loved you in another lifetime, because it feels like our souls are inseparable. You were made for me and I was made for you. I'm not a good man, but I'll always strive to be good to you. You deserve better than I am. But I'm a selfish asshole and I'll keep you anyway, because I'd rather die than spend a single day without you."

After the priest finishes his ceremony requirements, I hear the words I've been longing to hear since the moment I saw her standing in the doorway.

"I now pronounce you husband and wife, again. Luca, you may kiss your bride."

Without any hesitation, I take my wife in my arms and press my lips to hers and kiss her. I push my tongue into her mouth and slide it against hers, tasting her sweet flavor, while ignoring the noise from our small crowd. We walk hand in hand back down the aisle together, and make our way downstairs where we have food set up, as well as a DJ and a dance floor, because I intend to have a dance or two with my beautiful Athena. I get a whiskey for myself, and a sparkling white grape juice for my wife, since she can't drink. She stares at me with affection, and while I never expected any of this when I found her trying to steal from me, I welcome it.

I pull her over to a crowd of people to introduce her, because she shouldn't not know everyone at her own wedding.

"Butterfly, these are the De Luca brothers; Domenic, Dante, Drake, and Damian. And their lovely wives; Giada, Katherina, and Natalia."

She watches curiously, of course, noticing Dante and Drake both have an arm around Natalia. They all greet my wife, and I whisk her away to meet my other friends.

"This is Sin, Zade, and their wives; Kierra and Amira."

My wife smiles as she greets my friends, who I hope will become hers as well. She will see a fair bit of Sin, because if I travel for more than a day, she'll be coming with me. Athena will be spending a decent amount of time in Vegas.

I pull her away and she asks, "Are they mafia?"

Shaking my head, I say, "Sin and Zade, no. The De Lucas are a rival family, but we get along, and they are sometimes even friends. If there were ever a mob war to break out, I can guarantee you, they'd be on our side as we would be on theirs."

The music starts and I pull my wife into my arms where she belongs. She stares up at me as we begin to sway to the voice of John Legend singing 'All of Me', a song she said fits us perfectly, and I agreed.

Athena has one arm around my neck, while her fingers on her other hand stroke my cheek, as she stares at me with far more love than I deserve.

"I love you," she mouths to me.

"I love you too, Butterfly."

I kiss her softly as the song ends, and speak directly into her ear, "Come with me. I want to show you my wedding present to you."

I take her hand and walk her through the back of the house, and walk into one of the many bedrooms in our home, locking the door behind us.

As I unzip my pants, she gasps, "Luca, that is not a wedding present."

Dropping my slacks to the floor, I show her my erect cock, and she stares at me like I've lost my mind.

My wife focuses on my dick, and covers her mouth with shock, or horror, I'm honestly not sure which.

"You tattooed your dick, Luca? Are you crazy?"

I grin at her. "Crazy for you, baby."

She stares down at the blue butterfly, and her name inked onto my dick.

"Do you like it?"

Her cheeks are bright red as she admits, "It's insane. Normal people don't do this, but oddly, yes I like it."

Since she decided we weren't having sex again until we had our ceremony, it gave me time to get this tattoo done, and allow it to heal.

"Does it still hurt?"

I chuckle as I stroke my cock. "If you're asking if I'll be fucking my wife tonight, the answer is yes. Tonight and every night for the rest of our lives. And after our daughter is born, I'll put another baby inside you. There won't be a time when you don't have my cum dripping from your sweet cunt."

She squeezes her thighs together, and I grab her by the shoulders and push her down on the bed.

Athena giggles softly. "We have a house full of wedding guests."

I lift her dress over her thighs, and she spreads her legs. Pulling her panties to the side, I slide into my favorite place.

"I don't give a fuck about anyone else. All I see is you, Butterfly. You consume every part of me."

Hovering over her with a hand on either side of her, she bucks her hips up, as she places her hands in my hair and moans my name.

"Fuck, Butterfly, keep squeezing my cock like that, and I'm going to cum quickly."

She giggles. "That's okay, you can start over again, because I'll never get enough of you."

Athena took the words right out of my mouth because I feel the same way. Never in a million years did I think I was even capable of loving a woman. My feelings for my wife go far beyond something as tame as love. I'm obsessed with her. When I was a boy, my mother told me I couldn't keep a butterfly without killing it, but she was wrong. I'll keep this one. When I said I'd rather die than to spend a day without her, I was being sincere. My beautiful thief stole the one thing I never knew I had. *A heart.*

Epilogue Two

ATHENA

A whopping ten weeks after our daughter, Lucia was born, I found out I was pregnant, again. My husband was over the moon, to say the least, but I was not. It's not that I didn't want another baby, just not so soon. Things have a way of working out though, because as I stare at our almost one-year old daughter and cradle our newborn son, it's perfect.

I spot Luca crawling into the room, and Lucia squealing with delight as she attempts to walk to him, but she doesn't quite make it, and resorts back to a fast crawl. He scoops her into his arms and kisses her a thousand times, making her giggle. There is nothing better than the sound of your child's laughter. On the outside, people might assume that the head of a mafia family might not be capable of being a loving father. They'd be wrong. Luca is not only a wonderful husband, but a doting father. He is gone, working most days, but the second he comes into the room, our daughter's eyes light up. Of course, our son is younger and his only need beyond a clean diaper is my boob. Yet, I'm sure in time, he will be as obsessed with his dad as his sister is.

I'm still in therapy, dealing with the shit my father did to me. Maybe I will be for the rest of my life. When I get impatient with myself, she reminds me that the damage wasn't done overnight, and I won't be completely healed overnight either. It's a slower process than I'd like, but I've come a long way. I can read adult books now, which has quickly become one of my favorite hobbies. And the basement no longer freaks me out. Upon my request, Luca got rid of the cage months ago. The chains still sit attached to the wall, but those don't bother me as much. I've learned a lot about life.

Even the darkest days are preparing us for the beauty that waits for us to appreciate it. I wouldn't say I am glad for what my father did to me, but it did make me even more grateful for my life now. If I had to, I'd endure it all over again for the family I have now. When Luca found me, I instantly regretted following Manny's orders, and attempting to steal from a lethal mafia man. I had stolen many things for him, but this was my greatest job, because I gained more than any amount of money could ever provide.

Luca stares at me from the floor, while holding our squirmy daughter in his arms.

"We make really cute babies. We should make another one."

"Luca," I scold him, causing him to chuckle.

"Alright, we'll pretend. I'll shoot blanks, I promise."

He crosses his heart like he could really swear to such a thing.

"I don't think you have blanks."

The problem is, when he looks at me like he is, with a scorching stare, I know I'm going to lose the fight, because my husband does things to me. At this point, I'm a little concerned I'm going to end up with a hundred kids.

"Grandma is waiting for time with her grandbabies."

He stands up, scoops our son out of my arms, and winks at me. "I'll be right back."

When he comes back, he's surprised I'm still in the nursery and arches a brow. "What are you doing?"

I giggle. "Trying to figure out where we are going to put baby number three."

"We'll knock out the wall and make the room bigger."

I cross my arms over my chest. "Four, Luca. After we have four children, this obsession with getting me pregnant has to end."

He narrows his gaze at me and says, "Five."

Blowing out a long breath, I eventually agree. "Five, and you're done."

Walking over to me, he lifts me over his shoulder, making me squeal. "Five, and I'll get a vasectomy, because I'll never be done filling this pussy."

We make it to our bedroom, he kicks the door closed, and walks over to the bed and drops me onto it.

My husband stands staring at me with obvious heat in his expression.

"Beautiful Butterfly, until I can inhale your soul and connect it with mine, this is as close as I can get to you. It's when our bodies are connected that I feel most at peace. You are my peace. My salvation. My everything."

Climbing over me, he presses his lips to mine and pushes his tongue into my mouth. To others, he is a violent, lethal man. The one known to break bones to make his enemies suffer. To me, he is my husband, protector, and my greatest love. He was going to kill me, but instead, he saved me. Luca once told me that butterflies were beautiful and free, but I would never be free. I don't want to be. Like him, I'd rather die than to spend the rest of my days without him.

BONETTI BROTHERS

BOOK TWO

Reaper

A DARK MAFIA ROMANCE

CHELLE ROSE

Chapter One
REAPER

They never get away from me, only her. One might think she's smarter than the rest, since she escaped. Her one mistake was leaving her purse behind when she ran for her life, because now I know who she is and where she lives.

Arabella Riley.

Birthdate: May 21, 2005.

Address: 1624 Ninth Street, Apartment B4.

She made this so easy, and it makes me want to punish her. What if some other man had found this? Did she not consider how much danger she could be in?

I chuckle to myself because, of course, she's in a world of trouble once I get my hands on her.

They say the eyes are the window to the soul. It's the reason I do the things I do. Every set of eyes look beautiful as life evaporates from them. Arabella is the first I've wanted to keep the eyes from. I've already researched how to preserve them.

To preserve eyeballs, or any other organ or specimen, in a wet jar method, inject it with formalin. You'll want to inject quite a bit. Then place the injected specimen in a jar of the same solution of formalin for a few days or weeks. Even months, depending on the size of your specimens.

The problem for me is I don't only want them for weeks or months. I want to keep them forever. I never want those pretty blue eyes to fade away. Sometimes plans need to change. If she cooperates, maybe I'll let her live, so I can always have those pretty blues on me.

I sit in the club where she dances with her friends. Arabella dances as if she doesn't have a care in the world. Hands in her long blonde hair, swaying those hips like she's doing it just for me. Is she trying to taunt me?

Sweet, living dead girl. Tonight you will come face to face with the man that has become your greatest fear. You'll make a choice. Be mine or die. Either I'll get to see her eyes on me while I fuck her, or I'll look into them and squeeze the life out of her delicate body.

She stands between two girls, both brunettes, but I barely notice them. My attention is completely focused on living dead girl. Arabella tosses back her third drink of the night. Big mistake. She is going to need all her wits to get through the night, and the alcohol isn't going to help her. A man approaches her with a drink, and I'm done watching. I'm a Bonetti, and though I don't currently work with the family, my name still carries weight. I can do nearly anything I want to in this club, with little interference, including dragging Arabella out by her gorgeous blonde head of hair. And the fucker coming on to my girl? His night is going to be short, along with his life. What did he do to deserve to die? Touching what's mine is his crime. For that, he'll pay with his life.

I weave through the crowd of drunk gyrating assholes, spilling more than one drink, as I approach the douchebag, but not giving a fuck. Her back is turned to me so she has no idea I'm here. Stopping behind the blonde guy with his hand on her shoulder, I growl, "Get your hands off my property."

Arabella turns to the sound of my voice with a start, and instantly turns so pale she looks like a fucking ghost. A beautiful ghost. The fear in her eyes probably shouldn't make my dick anywhere near as hard as it does. Her ocean blue gaze widens, as I swear she has a cartoon bubble over her head saying, 'Run!'

I chuckle as I narrow my gaze at her. "Did you think I forgot about you, baby?"

The stupid man standing next to her glares at me, and asks her, "Do you want me to get rid of him?"

220

I laugh obnoxiously, because I'd really fucking like to see him try.

I grab his throat and squeeze hard, knowing he's freaking out because he can't breathe.

"This is how this is going to go. You're both coming with me, or I'll kill you right here, in front of God and everybody. The hundreds of witnesses won't deter me, because every cop in this fucking city is owned by my family."

My brother, Bones, is the head of the family, and killing two people with so many witnesses will definitely result in a lecture. However, he'd have my back the same way I'd have his. They glance at each other, and Arabella nods at her friend and says, "He isn't kidding. Do what he says."

I release blondie's throat, and order him to walk toward the back door and follow, watching them both closely. Living dead girl more than him, because fuck me, she's gorgeous. The only thing about her more stunning than her eyes, is that ass, that moves the exact right amount when she walks.

After opening the front door to my truck, I point for her to get inside before handcuffing her hand to the 'oh shit' handle, because I already know she's likely to run if she gets the opportunity. I push blondie into the back seat, zip-tie his hands behind his back, as well as around his ankles, and seatbelt him in, because safety is important.

I chuckle to myself after I close their doors, and make it to the driver's side and climb in. Arabella speaks as soon as I pull away. I love her voice, so soft and sweet, but she clearly thinks I'm an idiot. I know the part where you're supposed to humanize yourself with your would-be killer.

"My name is Arabella. I don't think we properly introduced ourselves before. I'm twenty-one. I work in a coffee shop, and I'm in college."

I turn out of the parking lot as she continues, "I'm young. I want to live. I'll do whatever you say."

Smirking at her, I say, "I knew all of that already, living dead girl."

She shifts uncomfortably in her seat with her arm stretched in the air. "What's your name?"

I glance in the mirror occasionally, watching to make sure blondie doesn't surprise me. It's hard with all four of your limbs restrained, but I've seen stranger things. His eyes are wide with terror, as he stares out the window like there's a way out. There isn't. Tonight he dies.

"They call me Reaper."

Arabella raises her eyebrow and asks, "What's your real name?"

I make a left turn, while I consider whether or not I should tell her. She isn't leaving alive, so it doesn't matter, especially because what will she do? Go to the police?

"Nico."

"Nico," she repeats, like she's trying my name out on her tongue, and I don't hate it. Somehow, I think any word coming out of her mouth would be sexy as hell. I make a mental note to make her beg. Fuck, I should put a metal collar around her slender neck, and walk her on a fucking leash. I've never done that before, but she makes me want to.

"Nico, please don't kill me."

I glare at her as I pull into the parking lot for the lake, in the middle of nowhere. That's why we're here, because I knew no one would be here at this time.

After putting the truck in park, I open my door, and whistle as I walk to her door and open it. Her blue eyes, filled with fear, stare at me and fuck, I've missed it. Rubbing my thumb over her bottom lip, I groan because she drives me crazy.

"Are you going to cry for him when he dies?"

"No," she whispers.

I take in all her features as I ask her, "Will you beg for me to spare his life?"

She shakes her head lightly. "I will only beg for mine."

Stroking my fingers down her cheek, I tell her, "If you want to prolong your life, you'll keep your eyes on mine while I extinguish his life."

This will be the first time I've ever not looked into someone's eyes while killing them, but I can't help myself. I only want to look at her.

I push her seat back, and grab her hips and rotate her, so she's able to see into the backseat. This is a test. A big fucking test. I'm about to see what my living dead girl is made of. If she screams and cries, then I know to kill her soon. If she shows me she's stronger than she appears, I might keep her a bit longer.

Acknowledgements

During the writing of this book, we lost a member of our book community that meant a great deal to me. Katie was a member of my ARC team for two years and even during her battle with stage four cancer, she was always a wonderful person. Katie was a librarian and simply loved reading. I hope she's somewhere peaceful, surrounded by all the books she loved. My heart goes out to her family, especially the beautiful babies she left behind. Fuck cancer!

To my ARC team:
Thank you for reading Bones ahead of release. It makes such a difference and I can't thank you enough.

To my Street Team:
You guys are amazing. Every time you share about my books, you increase my visibility in the world of difficult algorithms. Thank you.

To Chelle Rose's Filthy Girls aka my Beta/Alpha team:
To say I'm honored you choose to be part of this process would be an understatement. Every book you show up with excitement and comments that not only make my books better but keep me going. I adore each and every one of you! Heather, McKinley, Mariah and Carmela, you are amazing. Thank you for being on this crazy ride with me.

To my PA Grace:
Thank you for everything you do for me and for putting up with my special brand of chaos.

To my girl from RedFox Book Design:

I think this is book cover thirteen you have done for me. I adore you endlessly. XOXO.

To Furious Editing:
Thank you for the time and care you took with this book. I'm confident no comma was left behind. Here's to many more. Love you!

To the Reader:
Thank you so much for reading this book. I sincerely hope you enjoyed Luca and Athena's story as much as I loved writing it.

ALSO BY CHELLE ROSE:

Forbidden Desires Series

1. *Mercy www.books2read.com/chellerosemercy*
2. *Finding Mercy www.books2read.com/chellerosefinding-mercy*
3. *Liam and Mercy www.books2read.com/LiamandMercy*
4. *Xander's Secret https://books2read.com/Xanderssecret*

Dark Desires Series

1. *Unholy www.books2read.com/chelleroseunholy*
2. *Unhinged www.books2read.com/chelleroseunhinged*
3. *Unchained www.books2read.com/chelleroseunchained*
4. *Undone www.books2read.com/chelleroseundone*
5. *An Unhinged Wedding www.books2read.com/unhingedwedding*

Men of Mayhem Series

1. *De Luca: The Devil www.books2read.com/delucathedevil*
2. *De Luca: The Saint www.books2read.com/delucasaint*
3. *De Luca: The Sinister Game www.books2read.com/sinistergame*
4. De Luca: The Dalia Effect www.books2read.com/thedaliaeffect

Den of Sin Duet

1. Zade www.books2read.com/zade
2. Sin www.books2read.com/sin-chellerose

Bonetti Brothers Series

1.   Bones www.books2read.com/boneschellerose
2.   Reaper www.books2read.com/reaper-chellerose

Printed in Dunstable, United Kingdom

67172248R00139